FLOODWATER

Seay was looking down at the map when Bonal said, "Will you take the job?"

"What job?"

Bonal slowly raised in his chair. "You're to put the tunnel through. You've got to drive these buckos, fight with any weapon short of murder, fight without money, without enough men, and with a swarm of toughs and bankers taking turns at trying to down you." He rose and came over to the desk to face Seay. "I won't put a good face on it, Seay. Some interests in this ore-field won't stop short of murder to kill this tunnel idea. The men I can trust are few. You'll be one of them. The only thing I can do is pay you well, insure your life and depend on your loyalty. Is that enough?"

Seay nodded, still looking at the map.

Available in Fontana by the same author

Bounty Guns

LUKE SHORT

Floodwater

FONTANA / Collins

First published 1939
First issued in Fontana Books 1965
Second Impression May 1974

Printed in Great Britain
Collins Clear-Type Press London and Glasgow

Chapter I

Booming Tronah stepped up a pitch at six o'clock evening when the shifts at the mines came off and, like a great lusty and colourful caterpillar, turned over in the cocoon of its own din.

Charles Bonal regarded it from the open window of his suite in the Union House with something like affection tempered with disapproval, while behind him the waiter set a place for one at the massive desk in the middle of the huge panelled room. Bonal sniffed the faint hot breeze riding off the Piute sink. Its stink of sagebrush and sun on rock was fouled a little by the smoke and fumes of the stamp mills scattered to the east and south of the town, but it was there nevertheless, the all-pervading smell of the desert.

"All ready, sir," the waiter said, and Bonal nodded. Below him, in the dusk, the street was jammed with a continuous line of creeping ore wagons, nose of each lead team to the end gate of the wagon ahead, while around them and between them, almost oblivious to them, the noisy crowd milled. Three years of bitter complaint on the part of the merchants had never succeeded in re-routing to a side street this endless line of ore-freighters on their way from the mines to the stamp mills, for this was a boom town, and ore was king. Charles Bonal was glad of it for the two thousandth time.

He sat down in the deepening dusk to a lone meal, linen napkin under his short, bristly beard, and ate as ferociously as he talked and moved and thought.

He had lighted a cigar and poured himself an ample slug of brandy when the waited returned to clear the desk.

"Send my daughter in," Bonal said curtly, "if she can be spared."

He was squatting beside the small safe against the back wall when the door opened and Sharon Bonal entered. The noise of a party died out as she closed the door behind her.

"No lights again," she said reprovingly and stopped, and Bonal answered with a grunt. Crossing to the desk, she lighted the kerosene lamp, and by its glow saw her father raking sheafs of banknotes from the safe into a canvas sack. Observing him as she did now, he was a bent little man in broadcloth with a squarish head which had the set of a terrier's on his trim shoulders.

He said without looking around, "Having a good time?"

"Except for you being gone, Dad."

Bonal grunted again, but this time he turned around and laid his cigar on the edge of the desk, squinting from the smoke in his eyes. He was about to return to his business, when he looked up at her, and then, slowly, like a man treating himself to a rare pleasure, observed her carefully. Under his gaze Sharon backed away, picked up her full skirt and curtsied demurely, smiling. Her dress was of yellow silk, spangled with tiny blue cornflowers, and the wide neck and full short sleeves left her shoulders and arms bare, so that the sheen of her flesh contrasted to the dark wash of her chestnut hair. Only the slight dusting of minute freckles across the bridge of her nose saved her from regality—that and a kind of warm impudence in her blue eyes. For both Charles Bonal was thankful, for they were reminders of her maternity.

"Like it?"

"Yes. Yes," Bonal answered absently, and turned to the safe again.

Sharon said, "Is that money, Dad?"

"Have you lived in mining camps so long you don't know a greenback when you see one?" Bonal answered without turning around.

"Stupid. I mean, where is it going? And how did it get here?"

Bonal hefted the sack, slammed the safe door shut and stood up, tying the draw-string of the sack. He did not answer.

"You're going to gamble," Sharon said without reproof and with some interest.

"I won that last night. To-night I'll triple it—and I think I'll bring back something else." He walked over and took down his beaver hat from the antler hat-rack and put it on, so that it rode his head with an uncompromising squareness. Standing just out of the circle of lamplight, he watched his daughter a moment, scowling. She came over to him.

"The last night you'll be here, Dad. I thought we might spend it alone."

He gestured with his cigar towards the next room, the movement at once dry, ironical, explanatory.

"I'll send them packing if you say so."

"Why should you? I'll be busy."

She brushed a streamer of cigar ashes from the lapels of his coat, adjusted his bow-tie and gave the bottom of his waistcoat a yank, straightening out his pleated shirt-front, which had a tendency to creep towards his neck.

"Will you come in and say hallo?" she asked, smiling a little, making her voice purposely gruff in mockery.

He scowled. "They weren't asked in my name, were they?"

"You know they weren't. I wouldn't dare."

Behind his beard he smiled a little and removed the cigar from his mouth. "You would that. Good-night."

Downstairs, the lobby was thronged with men, and a cloud of acrid tobacco smoke billowed around the high chandeliers overhead. To Charles Bonal, who had known this town when it was a wild camp of tents and rock huts and brush shacks, this hotel was an irritating badge of Tronah. Though it was three storeys, it fronted on a street that was alternately bedded in six inches of muck or dust; though its hundred rooms had shiny new plumbing, only a third of them ran water; although its lobby and corridors had rolls of red plush carpet, bright paint, brassy murals, crystal, and gold braid, it missed elegance. It was typical of a camp whose boom had known no planning, whose gamblers possessed no shrewdness, whose foresight reached barely into to-morrow.

Making his way through this jam of men, Bonal was greeted on all sides with a quiet respect by the men in frock-coats and white shirts, and with a more jovial and deeper respect from the men in boots and corduroy. Without removing the cigar from his mouth, he nodded curtly, and all the time the sack of money was tucked under his arm as if it were ore samples, or even provisions.

On the street he turned into the tide of humanity which flowed over the board walk, letting it carry him down the street. It was only here that a man could best understand the lure of money, Bonal thought, as he submitted himself to the jostling, irresponsible crowd. Men of all nations, whose old country ways had not yet been filed down by the hard and fabulous life of this boom town, mingled here. Shallow-hatted Chinese cheek to jowl with smart and gaudy Mexicans, and stocky central Europeans rubbed elbows with Cornishmen, dour Welshmen and the ebullient, omnipresent Irish. Solid North-country Englishmen were here, to work out the remainder of their lives in the mines they understood. Germans, Canucks, Greeks, Jews—every race and every colour tramped these rotting board walks between the flimsy false-front shanties and stone buildings, for Bonanza was a word understood by the whole world. And through this stream, day and night, dominating and jeering and cursing, and liking it, were the Americans, a booted, hard-fisted, swaggering, hard-drinking, hell-raising mob, most of whom were ex-army men and tough to the core of their truculent souls.

Ahead of him, down this street which needed no light, there was a constant din, centred occasionally about the front of the saloons and gambling halls. The street was not lighted, for the lamps of a hundred business places had never acknowledged night. In the dust which moiled up from the unceasing feet of the freighting mules, there was another smell, whisky. It pervaded the work and play of this street with its fifty saloons, until it became part of the smell of sage and alkali and manure and powder-reeking ore and sweat and humanity.

Across the street, in front of the bright lights of Temple's Keno parlour, a man ballyhooed the games in a raucous, good-natured voice, designed to entice the miners away from their wages. And they went in, so that the entrance was clogged with them, for gambling was in the blood of this camp, and had built it. Bonal eyed them with a disapproval he did not voice, for in all this mass there was no one he could talk to.

He passed up a dozen saloons before he came to the Melodian, whose busy swing door of walnut fronted squarely on the street, so that every time a man came out he apologised automatically to the person who was sure to have been hit.

Inside, the over-sweet smell of whisky and fruits mingled with cigar smoke, but the crowd was not large. It was the best saloon in Tronah, patronised by the monied men, their mine and mill superintendents, and the better gamblers. At its rich mahogany bar only a dozen men engaged in conversation, for this was the lull at the dinner hour. No women were working here, which contributed to its quietness and air of sedateness. The wall seats were lined with leather, the waiters were in uniform, and the gambling tables towards the rear were ringed with chairs, a sure sign of calm in a feverish town.

Bonal took his brandy at the bar, talking idly with one of its customers until he felt a man come up beside him. In the bar mirror he saw the man, and beneath his beard there was again a small smile.

"'Evening, Mr. Bonal," Phil Seay said, and he was smiling too, as if there was an understanding between them, which there was. Taller by some eight inches than Bonal, younger by some twenty-five years, there was yet a look in his grey eyes that was similar to that on Bonal's. Seay owned the Melodian, and yet there was nothing about him that smacked of the tavern-keeper, none of that professional easiness of manner that did not distinguish the chaff from the wheat. On the contrary, there was a kind of sternness bred into that lean face which had not picked up its weather-burn from saloon air. The set of the frock-coat on Seay's over-wide shoulders was not right; it pinched at the shoulder seams, as if it was too tight, suggesting that he would be more comfortable without it. He moved with that stiff grace of a man who has spent much of his life in the saddle. His hands were long-fingered, square and bony when fisted, scarred in innumerable places, with a stiff brush of dark hair across the back of them which could not be as black as the trim-brushed hair of his head.

Bonal, regarding him in the bar mirror, nodded pleasantly, recalling all he knew of this man's brief history. A week ago Phil Seay had come to Tronah, and inside half an hour had picked up old acquaintances, veterans of a dozen gold camps of the past. They all knew him well; they all drank with him, and not so well. Early in the morning they had roistered as far as the Melodian. It was Phil Seay who went to the faro tables and quietly bought into the game. Inside an hour the faro banker had hunted up Morg Buchanan, the owner of the Melodian, with the news that his bank needed more money or the game must shut down. Morg Buchanan had taken over the faro bank himself. He kept it for exactly thirty-seven hours of straight playing, at the end of which time he had lost his money and the lease on his saloon and all its fixtures to the grey-eyed stranger with the run of luck.

That was his history, Bonal knew, and yet it told nothing about the man except that he knew how to crowd his luck. It was the quick judgment of him, his ruthlessness, his gambling and his stamina that Charles Bonal read into that winning streak, and he knew he had found his man. In that bony face, with its wide mouth and the deep-set, black-browed eyes, there was something that Bonal recognised and wanted and had to have. He could even do with the quiet mockery, which was in the eyes now and which was seldom absent from them.

Phil Seay said now, "Am I in for it again?"

"You are," Bonal said quietly. "As soon as I finish my drink, if it's agreeable to you."

"How many lickings do I have to take from you?" Seay asked.

"One more. Your last."

Seay smiled at this but said nothing. He had noticed the

canvas sack which Bonal had brought in, and he surveyed the tables at the rear. Presently, when Bonal had finished his drink, they went over to the faro table in the rear corner. A word to the house-man, and Seay had taken his place behind the table at the box. The four men idly gambling at the green cloth paid no attention to the change. It was only when Bonal, a cold cigar clamped in his mouth, hatless, the canvas sack on the corner of the table, started to play that their attention was aroused. Two of them dropped out to watch, but the other two played on, their small bets trailing Bonal's stakes.

Within an hour the saloon started to fill up, and the word soon got around of the game at the corner table. Another overhead lamp was brought by one of the waiters as the circle of watchers increased.

After two hours of play, when the other two players had been replaced by three more affluent men, Seay, who had been losing to Bonal and consistently winning back a tenth of his losses from the rest of the table, said, "Maybe you'd like a back room, Mr. Bonal?"

Bonal looked up. "Would you?"

"It's your pleasure."

"I'd like to stay here," Bonal said, and added dryly, "I'll trim you in public. I told you last night I would."

Seay smiled and said nothing, and the play went on. There was little conversation in the circle of watchers, for faro is a game of thought, demanding quiet. At a little after eleven Bonal called for a chair. At midnight Seay called for a box of cigars. At one Seay said, "If I've calculated right, Bonal, I'll have to close my house games for funds."

"Are you going to close this game?" Bonal asked.

"Certainly not. That was our agreement."

Bonal nodded. Seay called a house-man to him and talked briefly with him, then returned to the game. At a little past two, Seay said, "Now I'm down to the lease. Are you interested?"

Bonal raised his shrewd glance to him. "Depends. If I leave it, will you still try to operate the place?"

Seay smiled narrowly. "I don't like it much. If you'll accept it, I'll gamble it and the fixtures."

"Done."

At three, when all but the poker tables towards the front were abandoned, and the crowd at the bar had become larger and noisier, Bonal leaned back in his chair and regarded the chips in front of Seay. "I believe if I win this, you're through."

"That's right." Seay looked at him questioningly.

Bonal carefully lighted his cigar. "My boy, you've got several hundred dollars there—too little to do much with except gamble. You might even gamble well enough with it to start winning from me. Therefore I'm finished." He picked up his hat and regarded Seay placidly.

"Step in my office, will you, Mr. Bonal?"

"No. You cash in my chips and come with me, please," Bonal said calmly.

"But the lease?"

"We'll arrange that later. Come with me."

The chips were converted and Seay and Bonal left the Melodian. The crowd on the streets had thinned out somewhat, but the side-walks were still thronged, and the endless line of ore wagons rumbled their slow way down the street.

At the hotel Bonal led the way up to his suite and turned the lamp on the desk a little higher. While he got the whisky and glasses from the cabinet, Seay sat down and looked around him. He was facing the door, so that when it opened he saw Sharon slip through. For a moment they both stared at each other, and then Seay came to his feet, silent, his expression one of puzzlement.

Hand still on the door-knob, Sharon looked around her. She was in a grey wrapper, her tawny chestnut hair loose about her shoulders.

"Do you make a practice of walking into hotel rooms at night?" she asked quietly.

Over in the dark, out of the circle of lamplight where she could not see him, Charles Bonal chuckled. "This is Phil Seay, Sharon. My daughter, Seay." Then he added to Sharon dryly, "He came up because he was asked."

Sharon's face relaxed a little, and only then did Bonal understand that she had been genuinely frightened. She came across the room and nodded slightly to Seay, who towered above her in muteness.

"May I stay, Dad?" she asked.

"No. You can't even have a drink with us," Bonal said gruffly. "This is strictly business, dear."

Sharon came over and kissed him, and Bonal said, "I'll come in later, Sharon. Go to bed."

Sharon went back across the room. On her way she looked long, frankly at Seay, who returned the look with a kind of brash hostility before she closed the door.

Then Bonal ripped off his tie, pulled off his coat, hauled a chair around where he could put his feet on the desk, and sat with his hand cupped over the brandy glass. The cigar he offered Seay was refused, and while Seay drank, Bonal regarded him covertly.

"What do you do now?" Bonal asked finally.

"I'll see what your proposition is first," Seay said.

"How do you know I'm going to make you one?"

"You aren't the kind of a man who breaks a gambler for the fun of it," Seay told him quietly.

Presently Bonal said, "That's right. But you aren't a gambler, either," and he added, "I don't mean that offensively."

"I've been one for a week now—a good one."

"But not before that."

"No."

"You have no liking for it?" Bonal asked.

Seay looked at his brandy. "For gambling, yes. For being a gambler, no."

"Then you're not sorry I broke you to-night?"

Seay's quick smile was dry, amused. He said, "Bonal, are you trying to make me thank you for breaking me? Every man wants money. I want it too. There are other ways to make it besides gambling. I prefer them, I think, but when I began I didn't have a choice."

Bonal only grunted, and then he said abruptly, "I suppose you know I'm in the thick of a fight?"

"From what I hear, you always are," Seay replied.

"I don't mean that kind—quarrelling with mine shares, jockeying stock. That's a pillow-fight for a man with money. I mean a real fight." He paused and added bluntly, "A fight for survival." He gestured towards the table, where the canvas sack of bank-notes and gold still lay. "For instance, these winnings from you to-night will be sent by messenger to the coast to-morrow. Very likely this messenger will meet my creditors on the way to here." He smiled faintly. "Haven't you heard that, even?"

"I'm a working man, Bonal. That's my kind. We don't hear things you big augurs don't want us to."

"You resent it?" Bonal asked shrewdly.

Seay nodded faintly. "A little. But some day I'll be one of you and do the same thing."

Bonal smiled secretly. "Then you haven't heard that work on the Bonal Tunnel has stopped?"

"A rumour, yes."

"Well, it hasn't," Bonal said flatly. He drank off his brandy and rose and walked around the desk.

Talking, he moved the lamp over to the corner of the desk and from the bottom drawer drew out a heavy paper which unfolded into a map approximately the size of the desk-top. Seay rose and stood before it, a large-scale map of the Tronah section: and Bonal let him study it. Presently Bonal put a grimy finger on what appeared to be a large woolly caterpillar running north and south across the map, but which in reality was the Pintwater range, the group in whose eastern slope the Tronah gold and silver field was located. A dozen crosses in blue pencil located the town and principal mines on the slope. Bonal ignored these, and jumped to the other side of the mountains to place his pointing finger on a stream bed which paralleled the western slope. Where he placed his finger there was a red line which ran from the stream straight east half-way to the mountains. He said, "You've never been across, have you?"

"No."

"That red line," Bonal said quietly, "represents the Bonal Tunnel, a tunnel cut out of rock that is driving into the Pintwater range. So far, it has covered two miles and a half of the proposed distance of three and a half miles. It ends here." He pointed to the termination of the red line. "It will end here." He put his finger on a spot just east of the exact centre of the Pintwater range. "It will end there," he added grimly, "if I have to dig out the rest of it myself, and with a spoon."

While Seay studied it, Bonal sat down. His eyes looked tired, pouched with weariness, but the indomitability of them was unmistakable. A man of wisdom would have called Charles Bonal a fanatic, and he would have smilingly agreed and proceeded with his fanaticism. He did so now, his voice almost musing, but harsh.

"I've spent a week inquiring about you," he said abruptly. "You seem to have hit a good many gold camps. You've worked men, lots of men. But you're not an engineer. Is that right?"

Seay looked up from the map and nodded.

"You don't have to be an engineer to understand that tunnel," Bonal said. "But you have to understand human nature to know why it's necessary."

Seay said nothing, and Bonal hunkered down in his chair.

"When they started mining on this field," he said in a

harsh condemnatory voice, "they sunk their shafts where they found the ore—almost on top of the Pintwater range. When they got down to a depth of a thousand feet, they struck water. It filled their shafts. Instead of cutting up-casts to drain the water out, they bought pumps instead." He raised a warning finger to Seay. "Right now, they've got the biggest pumps invented in operation, and they're barely keeping the shafts dry. In another year the shafts will be so far down that no pump invented, no pump that ever will be invented, will be able to clear them of water."

"*Borrasca,*" Seay murmured.

"Exactly. *Borrasca*—pay out. There will be millions of dollars in gold and silver still in the ground—and it will stay there if I don't save the fools."

"How?" Seay asked curiously.

Bonal pointed to the map. "That tunnel. It starts on the other side of the Pintwaters. It will go straight into them and half-way through them to touch the very bottom of the deepest mine-shaft on this field. When it does, it will drain the water from these shafts and save the field." He chuckled, almost with pleasure. "Since these fools didn't ask for a Messiah, I'm giving them one. One with a beard too."

Seay was looking down again at the map when Bonal said, "Will you take the job?"

"What job?"

Bonal slowly raised in his chair. "The job of putting that tunnel through—superintending it. I can't be here. I've got to raise money. To-night I'm leaving for Mexico City. I've been refused loans from coast banks, from London, from Europe, from our own Government. Men are laughing at my scheme, but I've got to get money for it." He paused, watching Seay. "You're to put the tunnel through. You've got to drive these buckos, fight with any weapon short of murder, fight without money, without enough men, and with a swarm of toughs and bankers taking turns at trying to down you." He rose and came over to the desk to face Seay. "I won't put a good face on it, Seay. Some interests in this ore-field won't stop short of murder to kill this tunnel idea. The men I can trust are few. You'll be one of them. The only thing I can do is pay you well, insure your life and depend on your loyalty. Is that enough?"

Seay nodded, still looking at the map.

Chapter II

Sharon woke at noon and found Sarita, her Spanish maid brought from San Francisco, standing over her.

"How long have you been here?" Sharon asked.

"Ten minutes, miss."

"What time is it?"

"After twelve, Miss Sharon."

"Heavens. And I'm to have lunch with Hugh at twelve-thirty. Is he here?"

"Yes, miss."

Sharon rose on one elbow and looked around the room. Her clothes were laid out, and everything was in order. Still, the hotel room was depressing, and she lay back on the pillow after dismissing Sarita. Her conversation with her father at four o'clock this morning was still running through her mind. He had finished his business then, had wakened her to say good-bye and had talked for more than an hour sitting here on the edge of her bed. And in that hour she learned many things. She wondered if she was remembering them rightly, or if she had been so sleepy that she had things confused. Hadn't her father said that he'd hired a new superintendent—this man whom she'd met earlier in the evening—and that he was a professional gambler? Yet this couldn't be right. Sharon scowled and looked down at the bedspread. Yes, there was a smear of ashes that her father had dropped from his cigar, and the dirty marks of his boots where he had rested them on the edge of the bed, so she knew she hadn't dreamed it.

Throwing back the covers, she rose and walked over to her dressing-table, picked up her brushes and rang for Sarita.

It was a little less than an hour later when she appeared in the parlour of their suite. Hugh Mathias was standing there smiling, and she walked over to him and received his kiss on her cheek, and then said, "Good-morning, darling."

Her blue dress gave colour to that drab room, even to the neat black broadcloth suit that Hugh was wearing. Another man might have exclaimed over the dress, but Hugh Mathias did not. His frank blue eyes admired it, and Sharon understood and smiled back at him.

"You've been drinking," she said, pointing a finger at him.

"Customers. A machinery salesman this time. I'm going to

hire a secretary with a cast-iron stomach to receive my callers." Hugh grinned down at her. He was tall, and wore his clothes with the easy grace of a man used to fine living. He had a mobile, friendly face beneath a smooth cap of neatly groomed blond hair, and he looked as immaculate in his way as Sharon did in hers.

"I've ordered. Shall we eat here or downstairs?" he asked her.

Sharon said, "This is stuffy. Let's go down."

Once in the gilded dining-room downstairs, they were shown to a wall table, and Sharon looked around her. Immediately she smiled at this pretence of elegance. In San Francisco there was a beginning of fine living, and they had tried to ape it here. But the room smelled of cooked food, the waiters were unshaven, and it was easy to track a round dozen of the less well-dressed diners across the red plush carpet by the dirt they had left on it. The slovenliness of the frontier still stamped it.

"I'm sorry I was late, Hugh," Sharon murmured. "Dad came in just before he left and we talked till all hours of the morning."

"Was he sober?"

Sharon looked swiftly at Hugh, but the smile on his face took away the impertinence of his question.

"Of course. Why?"

"I've been hearing things."

"Like what?"

"Like this new superintendent. Have you heard it, or did he tell you?"

"He did," Sharon laughed. "And I've been wondering if I was sober when he told me. What have you heard?"

"Do you know him?"

"Met him."

"He's a gambler," Hugh said. "He owned the Melodian until your father won it from him."

"So that was it," Sharon murmured. "Go on."

"I'd hate to think your father would place a man like that in such a responsible position without knowing his background. I wonder if he did know it?" Hugh mused.

"Is it awful?"

Hugh shrugged. "Your father knows how to pick men—or says he does. This time, he's got a wrong hunch. Seay is a tough. He's notorious."

"A—a killer, you mean?"

Hugh nodded, and at the look of concern in Sharon's face, he said quickly, "Oh, not a camp bully or a renegade. He's hit every gold camp in the last ten years. He led the rush up the Frazer. He was at Reese River, Rawhide, Tonapah. He's built railroads, won and lost fortunes. He hasn't got a profession." He paused. "He's something of a legend among a certain class of people."

"What class?"

"Professional mining men, cowmen, railroad men." Hugh grinned. "Men that live by force, I should say."

"But the killings."

"I used the wrong word," Hugh said casually. "He's handy with a gun. I don't think he ever committed an unprovoked murder. Is that better?"

"It's bad enough," Sharon said, as the waiter brought their food. Hugh told her more. It seemed that yesterday Bonal had called on him, had told him of his intention to hire a new superintendent, and had asked Hugh to give all the assistance which he, as manager of one of the largest mines in the Tronah field, the Dry Sierras Consolidated, could give to the new man.

"So he'd been planning on it," Hugh said lightly, and shook his head, puzzled.

Sharon said nothing. This was as close as Hugh ever got to criticising her father, but she knew his feelings. Charles Bonal was playing for the largest stakes of his career, and things were going against him; now was no time to swap horses in mid-stream.

Sharon saw the desk clerk making his way across the fast-emptying dining-room to them. He paused at their table and handed Sharon a note.

"Mr. Bonal left this at the desk this morning, Miss Bonal. He said not to wake you to give it to you."

Sharon thanked him and opened the note, read it, and over her face was a look of annoyed amusement. "Speak of the devil," she said, and handed the note to Hugh.

He read:

Sharon—I forgot to mention the finances. Phil Seay is my agent here now. You'll have an allowance of two thousand a month. If it's necessary, go to him for more. Only go easy, honey.

Love,

C. Bonal.

"He wouldn't sign it 'Father,'" Sharon said, laughing a little. "That's too sentimental."

Hugh made a wry face and laid the note on the table. "Seay's your banker too, then."

"I don't think you like him, Hugh," Sharon said teasingly.

Hugh shrugged. "I don't like his reputation." He put down his napkin and tapped the note. "Darling, if you'll marry me now you can forget things like that."

"But I can live nicely on two thousand a month, Hugh!" Sharon protested.

"But why have to?" He leaned forward. "Don't you think I've waited long enough, Sharon?"

"Be patient, Hugh."

"But how can I? There's no end to this fight of your dad's. We'll both be grey when it's over." He laughed at her, but his eyes were urgent. "Do you *have* to wait, Sharon?"

"I promised Dad."

"Get him to absolve you. There's no reason why he shouldn't."

Sharon studied the table musingly. "You don't understand. When we're married, Hugh, Dad is going to rent five city blocks of San Francisco for the wedding party. He'll float a boat in champagne. He'll hire a private car to take us east. In London, Paris, Rome, Vienna, he'll rent whole floors of hotels." She looked up at Hugh with quiet appeal in her eyes. "Can't you see, Hugh? That's the way he wants to do it. He's contemptuous of money. That's his way of showing his contempt."

"And you?" Hugh said quietly. "Do you like the idea?"

Sharon smiled impudently. "I do. I think it would be fun. I think it would be fun because he'd think so."

"But it won't be his wedding trip!" Hugh said with quiet vehemence.

"You're wrong there, Hugh," Sharon said quietly. "It will be. It will be the last thing he'll ever force on us. I—I think I ought to allow him that. And he can't afford it now with his money tied up in this fight. Isn't it all very simple?"

Hugh shook his head in puzzlement and lighted his cigar. He looked at his watch, signalled to the waiter and said to Sharon. "I'll have to go, darling."

"But it's only three."

Hugh stubbornly stuck to his point, saying he was required at the mine, and saw Sharon to the foot of the lobby stairs, where he took leave of her. Climbing the stairs, Sharon wondered what she could do until dinner-time. In the afternoons she usually rode with her father, whose restlessness took him over the entire camp. She was suddenly lonesome without him, and just as suddenly reproved herself for it.

In the sitting-room she found a man dressed in a dark blue uniform of livery, and she recognised him.

"Hallo, Ben."

"Note for you from Miz Comber, Miss Bonal," Ben said, trying to hide the indelicate wad of tobacco in his cheek.

Sharon took the note. It was from Maizie Comber, and asked if Sharon could return with the messenger.

Sharon got a light wrap, too much against the heat of the desert afternoon, and went down into the lobby, preceded by Ben. At the hitch-rack a black red-wheeled top buggy hitched to a beautiful team of bays was waiting, and Sharon climbed in. Ben swung the buggy around into the stream of traffic, and they made their slow way north, heading out of town.

Immediately the heat of the desert sun drove through the buggy top and was all around her. She lay back in the cushions, lips parted a little for air, and watched this colourful parade. It was at times like this that she could not understand this boom camp of Tronah, nor her place here. Abruptly to the west, the gaunt and savage Pintwaters tilted to serrated peaks, their burned and scarified slopes like some gigantic sneer of Nature. There was colour here, but dark and ominous colour of tawny cinder and without a sight of the blessed green of foliage. The high mines up near the peaks she recognised by the jutting shelf of dump-heaps, but they were almost invisible unless an observer knew their locations. Here, then, was this strange camp of Tronah, a town sprung up on the very desert at the base of a desert mountain range. Water was piped thirty miles from the blue sierras to the west. Every stick of lumber, every bit of firewood, every bite of food—everything that went to make up life had to be freighted in here. It was not entirely real, Sharon thought sometimes, as she considered it. To the east, there was a vast expanse of rock and sand reaching half-way across a state. Only rare water-holes made it passable at all. To the south and the north it was the same, endless desert, different only in the gauntness of its rock and sand. Overhead, all day long, the sky was barren of clouds and the sun poured its thirsty heat down on everything alike, searing it, draining it of life until it was another part of this dead wasteland.

Later, when they mounted one of the many ridges, the town disappeared and there was nothing, save this rocky and rutted road, to indicate that man had been here. The desert swallowed it up, the long grey sage-stippled miles of sand and rock to the east meeting the rise of the foothills in an unbroken line.

Perhaps in defiance of this awesome sight, Sharon said, " Is Mr. Comber back yet, Ben?"

" Yes, Miz Bonal. He got back last night, late, I reckon."

" Too late to see Dad?"

" Yes, ma'am."

The road angled in towards the mountains here, and then fell abruptly into a little valley. The eye was drawn immediately and irrevocably to one spot in this valley, for here were three tall cottonwoods, the only green of this landscape. The house beneath them was only secondary, although it tried bravely to be the main attraction. It succeeded only in being defiant.

Of cut stone, masoned with the skill which only wealth can buy, it stood sturdy and square, three storeys, with a gallery running across the front, and white-painted gables jutting from its slate roof. A gravelled drive looped a wide fountain in front of the house where a thin stream of water rose high and fell upon itself in this still desert heat.

A woman was waiting on the porch, and when Ben wheeled around and pulled the team to a halt at the steps, the woman said gruffly, " Ben, you look at that pair of bays."

" Ben said, " Yes, Miz Comber."

" They look black to you?"

" No, Miz Comber."

" Why ain't the blacks hitched?"

Ben spat heartily and pushed his hat back off his forehead. He acted now as if he were used to this, and on more familiar ground. " Miz Comber, you can't keep a pair of high-blood horses like this penned up without they don't get fatter'n hawgs."

" Then use the brown buggy, you fool!"

" You tole me to take the black one."

" Brown with the bays and this one with the blacks!" Maizie Comber glared at him, and entirely without ill-feeling. She was a middle-aged woman with a pleasantly blowsy face holding deep lines of character incised beneath the flesh of easy living. Her hair, black shot with grey, was piled high on her head, and held a magnificent shell comb. Her gown was a gorgeous and elaborate affair of red silk, and down the front of it were food stains. A pair of easy-fitting and worn Indian moccasins peeped out from beneath its hem.

" Come in, Sharon, away from that old fool," she said bluffly.

Sharon was smiling as Ben, grinning sheepishly, helped her down. A monstrous fortune dug from the Tronah field had not changed Maizie Comber from the rough and good-natured wife of a rough and good-natured freighter. She was as plain as in the days when she used to water her husband's freight teams at the stage stop west of Placerville.

Following Maizie, Sharon walked through the foyer and into the wide hall that ran almost the length of the house. Inside was a kind of opulence that was breath-taking. Through the great double doors to the right, the oak parquetry floors stretched through three big rooms, the first a salon, and was brought up against the far wall of the third room where a great fireplace, flanked by tall fluted pillars of Carrara marble, rose almost ceiling high. This room was the library, where ordered rows of books, some of them collectors' items, filled three big walls. They were dusted weekly and never opened, for neither Abe nor Maizie Comber liked reading. The big salon held a great bronze piano with mother-of-pearl keys. On the far wall was a Romney portrait, untastefully flanked by two huge tapestries, one depicting the story of the prodigal son, the other the siege of Troy. Frail gilded chairs were grouped about the wall. A vast mirror, edges a gilded writhing of rosebuds, covered the wall opposite the piano. The windows, of French plate-glass, were hung with Venetian lace and blinds. Overhead, twin crystal chandeliers glittered, while yards of oriental rugs underfoot almost subdued their elegance.

The other rooms were like these, rich, expensive—and tasteless. Maizie padded down the corridor, oblivious to it all, and opened a door which let on to a small corner room. Sharon caught sight of a woman just rising out of a chair in front of a table holding a silver tea service.

"Beulah, pick up them tea traps and clear out," Maizie said. "Bring some more." The servant rose and started to clear the table, and Sharon glanced obliquely at Maizie. But Maizie was unashamed of the fact that she had been discovered taking tea with her servant, and Sharon loved her for it. This room was as simple as Maizie's simple tastes could make it. The chairs were old, comfortable, and the mahogany secretaire in the corner was scuffed and unpolished. The rug was plain and worn and the only pictures in the room were photographs of the old Petersburg mine, where Abe Comber had made his money. Moreover, the room had the air of being lived in, held the smell of food, of perfume, of tobacco and of dust.

"Sit down, honey," Maizie said, waving Sharon to a chair.

" Ben said Abe got back last night," Sharon observed.

" Drunk," Maizie said laconically. " Somebody sold the old fool a lumber business out on the coast too."

" Dad will be sorry he missed him."

Maizie sniffed. " He will not. Nobody's sorry when they miss Abe Comber drunk."

" Maizie, you know that isn't true," Sharon protested. " He drinks too much, but then all our men do."

" It's not the drinkin', it's the wakin' up," Maizie growled. " He's too old to carry on like that, Sharon. A body can't live with him. This mornin' he faunched around like a crazy man until I drove him out of the house."

Sharon laughed in spite of herself, but Maizie ignored her.

" That's what I called you over about."

" What?"

" Sharon, I've got to send my orders for next week's party off on to-night's stage. I talked it over with Abe at breakfast. Everything went along fine until I asked him how much champagne to get. Then he was mad." Maizie got up, threw out her chest and took long strides across the floor, talking in a deep, gruff voice that mimicked her husband's. " 'Woman, champagne is a damn' swill made for Frenchmen. No self-respectin' American would drink it, and I won't have it served in this house. The only liquor I serve here is whisky, good American whisky, rye preferred. If it's good enough for me to drink, it's good enough for my guests.' "

Maizie paused and glared at Sharon, her kind old eyes angry, and then she suddenly smiled. Sharon laughed outright.

" Whisky for women," Maizie observed grimly. " A foreign opera star as the guest of honour, and I'm to serve her a hooker of rye whisky." She crossed the room and sat down and called, " Beulah!"

There was a rustling behind the door and the knob turned and the servant entered, placing a tray of tea things on the table.

Maizie poured two cups of tea, gave one to Sharon, poured her own out in the saucer, took it up in both hands and blew on it.

" What do you want me to do, Aunt Maizie?" Sharon asked.

" What do you like in this house?" Maizie countered.

Sharon frowned. " What do you mean?"

" I mean, what gadgets in this house do you like? Any rugs? Any of those gimcracks out in front? Do you like any of 'em?"

" Of course. Why?"

" Then I'll sell any of 'em to you. In return, I want two

thousand dollars." She murmured into her saucer, "I'll show that old fool!"

"Is it money you want, Aunt Maizie?"

Maizie nodded. "We fought. I told him I'd order champagne and he said I wouldn't. He said he wouldn't give me any money and that he was ordering the rye this morning."

Sharon set down her cup of tea and laughed until tears were in her eyes. Toward the end, Maizie laughed too, but her grim old fighter's face had not surrendered one jot of conviction.

"I'll lend you the money, Aunt Maizie, but there's no use of selling any of your belongings." She wiped her eyes with her handkerchief. "Besides, Abe will have forgotten it in two days."

"Of course he will, but it'll be too late to get the champagne here. Then he'll be mad because we haven't anything to drink except that hogwash that he'll be able to pick up at the saloons. I know him."

"Can I have Ben for a couple of hours?" Sharon asked.

Maizie again yelled, "Beulah!" and when the servant appeared, said, "Tell Ben to come here."

Sharon borrowed pen and paper and wrote a note: "Will you please give bearer two thousand dollars immediately. Sharon Bonal."

When Ben appeared she gave it to him and said, "Do you know Phil Seay?"

Ben's wary face broke into a smile. He said warmly, "Hell, yes. Who don't?"

"Ben!" Maizie said sharply.

"Yes, Miz Bonal," Ben said humbly.

"Will you take this to him over at the Tunnel, Ben? Wait until he gives you a package and bring it back to me here."

"And you'll ride a saddle-horse," Maizie put in.

Ben took the note and went out. Two hours later he was back at the Comber mansion and was shown into the dining-room, where Maizie and Sharon were eating from solid silver service.

He gave Sharon the note, and she opened it, frowning a little as she noticed that the note was the only thing Ben carried.

The note said: "I will not. Phil Seay."

Chapter III

Ben had been gone an hour. Phil Seay shoved his plate away from him and reached for his pipe. Suddenly the heat of this tiny mess hall was too much for him, and he rose, stepped over the bench and went outside to lean against the door-jamb. The thin cotton shirt he wore was even too much for this heat, and the high boots he was wearing were hot and uncomfortable.

The rocks still held the heat of the day, but a faint breeze stirred off the slope hard to the east. Dusk was just lowering, blurring the hard shape of the mountains into a more kindly form. From his position in the door he could hear the hammering clatter of pots and pans in the cookshack just off the small mess-room, and as a counterpoint to this din, there was the roar of the big mess hall on the other side where the hundred workmen were eating now.

He raised his gaze up the slope a little. There, already lighted by a dozen kerosene flares, was the entrance to the Tunnel, and he could see into its depths a ways until the angle shut off sight. As he watched, four mules emerged from the Tunnel, dragging a string of loaded ore cars behind them. Their pace quickened as they came down the slope and took the slight run up to the dump heap where the dump crew blocked the wheels of the cars and dumped them. The lanterns hung on the collars of the mules winked dimly in the dusk. As the cars passed the tunnel mouth, a team of mules dragging a string of empties had cut in from the spur track and disappeared plodding into the tunnel mouth. The night was silent then, except for the steady hammering thud of the compressor pumping air into the receiving tank for the drills at the tunnel head. Down by the dry stream bed in a huge corral, a fight started among the mules and then stopped, and Seay had a swift picture of the beasts eating after the day's work, impatient with the heat and the work.

It lay spread before him, all the machinery of this complicated mechanism, and it was his to drive. Over across from the mess hall, he knew the exhausted men would be dragging to the bunk-house to tumble in their beds, worn out from working at the tunnel heading in one hundred degrees of heat. Somehow, this camp had a sodden air of stubbornness, but only that. The fight, the drive was lacking. He knew the feeling well; it was a feeling bred by hopelessness, when men work only for wages and not for a goal. Already, in the minds of these workmen, the tunnel was abandoned. It was only a matter of time until they would be laid off. This was the thing he had to fight. All this day, he had watched these men as he pried silently into every corner of this sprawling outfit. He had asked questions whose answers he did not comment upon and each man had eyed him, not with hostility exactly, but taking his measure. A new man Bonal brought out to break, he could almost hear them say.

Beyond him, he heard a man rise and leave the table, and the sound of footsteps paused behind him. He looked around. It was Reed Tober, the assistant superintendent.

"We'll pull this shift off at midnight," Seay said.

There was no answer, and it irritated him. Tober he knew was not yet through sizing him up, and although he admitted to himself that in Tober's place he would have kept his silence until he knew his man, still this passive and non-committal submissiveness angered him.

"You hear?" he asked, almost sharply.

"Why?"

Seay glanced up at the man. Framed in the doorway, the light behind him, Tober might have been stamped out of leather. His face was burned blacker than his dark hair, so that the whites of his eyes gave him a perpetually staring look. Slight of built, not so tall as Seay, he had that leaned-down, long-muscled grace of a racehorse. His face was a Texas face, with thin, tight muscles stretched under the skin of it. It was bony without being cadaverous, intent without being fanatic, and held that quick, febrile intelligence seen sometimes in a good bird-dog. To disguise the possibilities of that face, Tober moved with a lazy indolence that held the explosive threat of a coiled spring. To a man not acute of perception, Reed Tober was as unreadable as the back of a playing card. Right now, he was studying Seay with calculating, questioning intensity, and Seay knew that he was going to break this man's reticence tonight. For Reed Tober, assistant to a round half-dozen harried and bedevilled superintendents, had outlasted them all. He would outlast Seay, or so his tone implied.

"I'm laying a double track down before the morning shift," Seay said. "There's room in the tunnel, isn't there?"

"Not much to spare."

"Equipment? Track?"

Tober turned and said quietly, "Kelly." A stocky man with

a longhorn moustache and the brawny arms of a mine worker came to Tober's side.

"Pull this crew off the head at midnight. Rip up that spur track and measure it, and measure the dump track too. Check the track in the warehouse. If you're short, roust out a crew of teamsters and go freight some rails from the Golgotha. If the watchman won't give it to you, go round to Miss Vannie Shore's place and tell her you're from Bonal. I want enough to make a double track that will clear the tunnel mouth by a hundred feet. I want it in by six—and working."

Kelly stepped out past Seay and was gone into the night.

Seay said to Tober, "Why wasn't that done before?"

"Money," was Tober's laconic answer.

"About this upcast," Seay went on coldly. "You've got two from the slope down to the tunnel already, but it's not enough ventilation. You're past due putting one in now. Those men are working in close to a hundred degrees of heat. Where's your next upcast?"

"I'll put a crew on it to-morrow."

"Why isn't it in there now?"

"Money," was Tober's answer again.

Seay removed the pipe from his mouth with an impatient gesture. "Money, hell. You're working six shifts of four hours each in the tunnel head now. Put an upcast in there and you could work three eight hour ones. Isn't it cheaper?"

"Labour's cheap. Drills and powder and rigging cost money—or so Barnes thought."

"Barnes is gone. I'm boss here now. Put the upcast in. Order a couple of Root blowers from the coast to-morrow."

Tober only nodded. It went on like this. With a brutal disregard for the other man's feelings, Seay ticked off the changes, never failing to ask why they hadn't been done before. He found that Tober had planned most of them, knew how to make them, knew their costs; and the reason they hadn't been done was always the same: money. Cruickshank, the engineer, Peters, freighting super, and Hardiston, the grey little bookkeeper, all left the mess hall, walking between Seay and Tober, and not once did Seay stop. He could feel the edge mounting in Tober's voice, could feel the cold rage of the man, and it pleased him.

Finished, he was silent. His pipe had died. He struck a match, lit up, then said pleasantly, "All right. I've told you what's got to be done. Now tell me how much money I have to do it with."

"None," Tober said quietly, then amended this, "or close to none."

"Let's see the books."

Together, they skirted the mess hall and came out into the rough street on which the half-dozen buildings fronted. Tober tramped silently past the bunk-house and stopped at a rough slab shack at its end. He unlocked the door, lighted a lamp, and Seay looked around him. In one corner was a high desk littered with draughtsmen's tools, in the other the high desk of the book-keeper. Two deal chairs were against the wall. Tober opened the door in the far wall, and with lamp in hand entered. This room was almost as spare as the first. It had a low desk against the wall, and a wreck of a swivel chair was pulled against it. A squat square safe huddled against the far wall. There were two other chairs in the room, a calendar, and a run-down clock.

Putting the lamp on the desk, Tober knelt before the safe and opened it. He drew out a ledger, which he laid on the desk, looking evenly at Seay as he did so. There was good-humoured malice in his eyes.

Seay swung a leg on to the desk. "Sit down, Tober."

Tober pulled out the swivel chair and sat down. Seay ran a musing hand over the ledger, his grey eyes speculative.

"I've had this job less than twenty-four hours, Tober. I've been pretty rough to-night, haven't I?"

Tober only nodded.

"I've been in this town less than two weeks, I've picked up gossip, a lot of it bad, about Bonal. I talked to him last night for three hours. I didn't find out much." He looked at Tober. "How does Bonal stand now?"

"He's strapped."

"I know that. But what's he fighting besides lack of money? Who are his enemies, and how do they fight?" He paused. "I know what's got to be done here. I want to know what's got to be done away from here."

Tober relaxed a little. He cuffed his Stetson off his forehead and reached for a thin cigar in his shirt pocket and lighted it, then exhaled slowly.

"Know how this tunnel started?"

"No."

Tober told him how Bonal had conceived the idea, and how he had put it before all the mine owners. Bonal's scheme was to start his tunnel on the other side of the Pintwaters, dig straight into them, and touch the mine shafts when they had reached a depth of some two thousand feet. He was to drain these shafts of the water that was flooding them, and in turn would collect two dollars for every ton of ore that the mines raised from ground drained by his tunnel.

"But he needed cash to swing it," Tober went on. "So he went around to all the mines and got them to subscribe to part of the cost of the tunnel."

"Then he's already spent their money?"

Tober said wryly, "He never got any. They signed up to subscribe, and then broke their contracts." He studied his cigar thoughtfully. "You can buy any jury in this district, you know. The court claimed the contracts weren't legal."

Seay was curious now, watching Tober's face. He knew all this was preliminary to answering his first question, as to who was fighting Bonal. He said then, "But the tunnel is sense. Couldn't these mine owners see that?"

"Ever hear of Janeece?" Tober countered.

Seay nodded. "He owns a couple of reduction mills here."

"He owns them all," Tober corrected him. "He's the man that killed the tunnel."

Seay scowled. "How did he?"

"Laughed it to death," Tober said curtly. "Janeece understood one thing about this tunnel, I reckon—that when it went through, his business was finished. These mines, instead of hoistin' their ore a thousand or so feet and then freighting it five miles to his reduction mills, would shoot it through Bonal's tunnel and down to the reduction mill Bonal aims to build yonder on the river bank. Janeece saw if the tunnel went through he was done for, and he tried to kill it."

"But how?"

"Janeece's mills are backed by the Pacific coast banks—to begin with. Of course, they wouldn't loan Bonal any money. Then Janeece, to boot, bought into several mines in the Tronah field and started the rumour the tunnel couldn't be put through. He got engineers to swear to it. Herkenhoff—he's the manager of the Pacific Shares mine—is an agent of Janeece's. He broke his contract with Bonal. The rest did the same. And Bonal didn't get a cent from them." Tober shook his head slowly and dropped his cigar on the floor. "Bonal's a fighter, but even a fighter's got to eat."

Seay rubbed a hand over the ledger, back and forth, watching his hand. "What does this Janeece look like?"

"It don't matter," Tober drawled. "You'll never see him. He works through a dozen men. Without ever leavin' his office there at his big mill, he's killed Bonal's credit all over this country." Tober was about to elaborate, but he only said briefly, "Men work for him, that's all."

"But what kind of men?" Seay insisted.

Tober's gaze swung up to him and regarded him thoughtfully. "Men like Chris Feldhake, for one. Herkenhoff for another. But Feldhake is the dangerous kind. He'll do anything for money—from a killin' to a bribe."

Seay said nothing, thinking, and Tober said quietly into the silence, "You better pack a gun from now on, Seay."

"Why?"

"Because," Tober said steadily, "I think you can swing it. I think Bonal's found his man. And if he has, there'll be trouble—real trouble. And it won't be with banks and loans now. It'll be the other kind of trouble."

Seay looked at him a long time and then dropped his gaze. "Thanks," he said.

Tober said nothing.

"How much money have we got?" Seay asked then.

"Not enough to meet this week's payroll," Tober answered. Their glances met. Seay scoured his face with a hand and then smiled a little, finally laughed shortly. Tober rose now and went over to the safe, and after opening it pulled out a large cashbox and laid it on the desk. "All we got is in there," he said quietly.

"Let's count it, then."

Tober opened the box, and then, his hand still on the lid, paused and looked up at the door. Seay turned. In another moment someone entered the other room.

A sudden flood of anger swept over Seay. This was a woman's step.

Chapter IV

Sharon Bonal stood in the doorway. Seay looked at her a long moment, and then took off his hat. Tober grabbed for his too, his face surprised out of its impassiveness.

"Good-evening," Seay said quietly.

Sharon nodded briefly. "Is there any place we can talk?" she asked.

Seay looked at Tober and Tober tramped stiffly across the room, past Sharon, and out.

Seay motioned to the swivel chair, but Sharon seemed not to notice it. There was an expression of cold pride in her face as she said, " I want that note explained."

" It explains itself," Seay answered quietly.

" Are *you* to tell me how much I'm to spend?" Sharon asked quietly.

" It seems that way."

" On whose authority? My father's?"

Seay said quietly, " Sit down, please. This will take some time." He stood motionless, his tall figure stamped with a kind of ruthless dignity as he waited for her to move. The lamp flame guttered a little with a sudden stir of hot wind, and then Sharon swept across the floor to the swivel chair, Seay's gaze following her with a wary curiosity.

He sat down on the desk then, one leg over the corner. " If your father's memory hasn't failed him, he put two thousand dollars to your account the first of this month. This is the eleventh," he began quietly.

Sharon said, " I want two thousand dollars. The subject of my money is no business of yours, even if you seem to make it."

" You won't get it." Seay's voice was hard, final. " If you won't be reasonable, there's no reason why I should."

Sharon hated him then, and he could see it in her eyes. He also observed the colour creep into her slim throat and up into her face, and he waited quietly for the blow-off. It didn't come, for Sharon's reply was temperate, almost apologetic.

" Maybe I have been a little high-handed, but you can hardly blame me. Father turned over all his affairs here to a perfect stranger, then skipped out to Mexico City. I think your note was insolent, but then that's a matter of opinion." She paused, getting Seay's nod. " It happens that Dad has given me money this month. It also happens he told me to go to you if I needed more—and I do need more."

Seay smiled thinly. " This is a boom camp, Miss Bonal. Food is pretty high—about three dollars for a good meal. A cheap hotel room is double that, and a good one about five times that. But it happens your food and rooms are paid for. I made sure of that last night." He added dryly, " That leaves two thousand for entertainment. Enough, isn't it?"

" I want this money for a loan," Sharon said coldly.

Seay shook his head. " That's too bad. Your father is fighting for loans too. He borrows money, you loan it out. It doesn't work."

Sharon kept silent, studying the hard and ruthless face of him. There was a touch of mocking humour behind those grey eyes, but the long and sober face showed only a granite stubbornness, which only served to strengthen Sharon's own. Still, she had enough earthly common sense to know that this was not a man like Hugh who, at the first sight of a woman's displeasure, gallantly gave in.

Seay was saying, "As long as I haven't been minding my business, I'll step out of line once more. Is the loan for a person in need?"

Sharon considered. "Yes," she said honestly.

"A friend of yours and your father's?"

"Of course."

Seay said carefully, "Would less money do?"

"I think not."

"If it's financial trouble, you're being too generous. Your own father has enough of that kind. But if it's for a needy person, I should think you could spare a hundred or so from your allowance. If you can't, I can lend it to you."

"Two thousand dollars," Sharon repeated firmly. "And I've got to have it before the night stage."

Seay's eyebrows raised a little. "Someone leaving?"

Sharon nodded imperceptibly, and Seay rose. "All right. I'm going over to Tronah. I'll go with you to see this person," he said, his eyes steady and watchful.

Sharon made an involuntary movement of protest, and then she knew she was trapped. "I lied," she said stubbornly. "Nobody is leaving. It's for an order that has to go out on the night stage."

"Ah," Seay said quietly. "Now we're down to it. An order for what?"

Sharon raised her furious gaze to his. "You didn't believe me?"

"I don't believe you know anyone in need," Seay said frankly. "You'd avoid knowing them. An order for what?"

"Champagne!" Sharon said sharply, stamping her foot. "There, you know it! Maizie Comber's husband has refused to pay for the champagne Maizie must order for a party. He's threatening to make her serve rye whisky. I offered to lend her the money!" Her eyes were blazing. "Is there anything criminal in that! Trying to help a friend?"

Seay shook his head and said gently, "It's no dice. No, you can't have the money. And good-night, Miss Bonal."

"But I promised her!" Sharon said angrily, rising. A note of pleading now mingled with the exasperation in her voice.

Seay looked long at her, his fist clenching unconsciously. Impulsively he reached over and flipped open the top of the cashbox.

"Maybe I'm a little unreasonable," he drawled softly, pointing to the neat stack of ragged bank-notes in the box. "There's a little over twenty-five hundred dollars in that box. We meet a payroll of four thousand to-morrow. Your father's in Mexico City. My job is to drive this tunnel through and that's all the money he left me to do it with." His hand dropped to his side. "Maybe you can tell me how I'll meet the payroll this week, let alone next week. Maybe"—and his voice carried the overtones of savage scorn—"you'd like to lend me two thousand dollars from your allowance, so I can meet the payroll."

Sharon felt her face go hot.

"Maybe," Seay went on brutally, "it won't do any good. Maybe Bonal's whole scheme will cave in on him." He finished bluntly. "Times like this, I hope it does. You might find then how easy it is to pour a man's blood and bones and soul down the throats of your friends, and still have them call it champagne."

Sharon brushed past him to the door, and was almost through it when she stopped and turned. "It might be a good idea for you to leave, Mr. Seay. Father will be in San Francisco to-morrow, and I'm going to the telegraph station now."

"Yes, it might be a good idea," Seay conceded. He heard her go out, heard the murmur of voices, and then the trotting of a team of horses which was soon blotted out by the deep silence of the room.

Seay looked down and found that his fists were clenched, and he unfisted them, his gaze on the box. Slowly, reason took over his brain again, and the anger died, leaving only a rooted contempt for this woman. Striding over to the desk, he looked down at the cashbox. He thought he understood Bonal now, and there was no anger toward him. Bonal had succeeded thus far by hiring men and sucking them dry, by placing on their shoulders a burden whose enormity crushed them. Like this here, now, before him. All that held Bonal's tunnel scheme together now was himself, Phil Seay, a gambler, a stubborn man, a new man, and he had something less than twenty-four hours in which to effect a way. Bonal, with that shrewd and ruthless judgment that could gauge to a nicety the precise mixture of vanity and pride and ability that drove a man, had named his man and left him to fight it alone. If Seay won this time, there were other fights. When he lost one, he would go the way Barnes went, and the way of the other five superintendents. It was a hard game Bonal played, and it took hard men to back his hand.

Seay turned away from the box, smiling a little to himself. He paced slowly around the room, his restlessness kindled by the knowledge that this box on the desk held failure for him—failure before he started. Still, if he could meet to-morrow's payroll and the next, still ramming this tunnel on and on into the Pintwaters, he knew that Bonal would not fail him. All Bonal wanted was a man who wouldn't let him down.

Seay turned his head abruptly and looked again at the box, his breath held. Then he turned to the safe, rummaged inside it and brought out a canvas sack. It was the work of only a few moments to stuff these banknotes and gold into the sack, put the empty box in the safe, lock the safe, blow out the light and lock the building behind him.

Tober was waiting outside, leaning against the bunk-house, smoking in moody silence.

"Have a horse saddled for me, Reed," Seay said, and walked past him and into the bunk-house. Tober stood motionless, watching Seay's back. Then he smiled into the night, his thin, secret smile, dropped his cigarette and headed for the corrals.

Inside the bunk-house, Seay turned up the overhead lamp and went over to his bunk in the corner. From underneath it he dragged out his small trunk and lifted it to the bunk. A moment later he drew out a Colt .44, spun its chamber and felt its loaded weight under his fingers and rammed it into his hip pocket and went out, his heavy boots curiously soundless on the scuffed floor.

From the low pass over the Pintwaters between Tronah and the tunnel, Seay could look down on the sprawling camp below him, its lights drifted across the slope in a careless swarm. Beyond it, closer to the flats, he could pick out the reduction mills, their great chimneys lifting flame up into the night. Raised a pitch above the murmur of the town's activity was the rhythmical pounding of the stamps in the reduction mills. Night and day, this hungry camp was slowly gutting the earth of this mountain, packing out and sorting its treasure with that stubborn patience of which only men and ants are capable.

Seay reined up and regarded it, and he felt a swift and

impersonal pride in all this; and he looked beyond it to the starshot void of the desert, and he was humble then.

Above him and far to the left on the invisible mountains, were pinpoints of light from the mine offices. Occasionally he could catch the flicker of dim lights descending the mountain and he knew these were the ore freighters, with lanterns on the collars of the lead mules.

Late, he found Tronah teeming as usual, its streets rowdy with its life. Stabling his horse at a feed corral on the edge of town, he moved up the jammed sidewalk.

At Jimmy Hamp's Keno Parlour, he left the street and went inside. The reek of beer and whisky and tobacco and smoke and sweat and cheap perfume was rank and clamorous, and as it hit him he winced, patiently working toward the bar. This was the miners' saloon, as frank and big and bawdy as its roughest patron. At the crowded bar he waited, a high, quiet man, for his drink, and when he was served by the harried barkeep, asked after Jimmy Hamp. Hamp was back at one of the tables, the bartender said.

A dance hall girl at a table saw Seay and waved, and Seay nodded, knowing it was useless to try to speak above the din. Somewhere in the rear on the edge of the dance floor, a piano ground out an insane din that nobody listened to.

Jimmy Hamp was watching a poker game, his swart, utterly bald head beaded with drops of perspiration. He had most of a cold cigar chewed up into a ball which he cuddled in his mouth, and its fetid stench settled around him like an aura. He saw Seay and put out his hand and tried to talk and then shook his head, grimacing.

He beckoned Seay to a door in a wall at the far end of a bar. Half-way there, a row started back on the dance floor and there was a quick scuffling of feet. A bouncer fought his way to it. Jimmy directed a worried gaze in that direction, but his height was against him and he could see nothing but a tangle of milling shoulders and heads. He shrugged and Seay followed him to the door, and they both went into the office.

"Honest to God, Phil, what I need is a corral with a roof on it," Jimmy said wistfully after he shut the door. He shook Seay's hand again and motioned to a chair.

"Business good?" Seay asked.

Jimmy said, "Too good. If it keeps up, I'm goin' to give the drinks away. I can't collect for half 'em now with this mob." He eyed Seay with friendliness and sat on the desk. "Heard you got took."

Seay hunkered down in his chair and pulled out his pipe, nodding.

"Well, you landed on your feet, you son-of-a-gun," Jimmy said, smiling. "You never belonged in this business anyway."

"That's what Bonal thought."

"A Big Augur now, hunh?" Jimmy murmured. "Well, it don't take you long, Phil. You started at Reese River with a half dozen teams and you wound up on top of the heap."

"Broke."

Jimmy laughed and dropped his cigar into a spittoon. "Who didn't?"

They chatted of Reese River a few moments, and when a pause occurred Seay asked, "Where's the big game to-night, Jimmy?"

Jimmy regarded him shrewdly and slowly drew out a cigar from a pocket of his open vest.

"You mean the giant-killer?"

Seay made a wry face and shook his head. "I never sat in a game where the white chips come at a hundred. I wonder how it would feel," he mused.

"Ask Abe Comber."

"Maybe I will," Seay murmured. "No, I'm looking for a high limit where a man can have ambition."

"That's hard to find in this man's town."

"That's why I came to you. If there is one, it's floating. Where is it to-night?"

Jimmy took out his cigar and studied its tip with frowning concentration. Then he raised his glance and said, "In the back room here."

Seay laughed. "I didn't think you'd let a white shirt in the place, Jimmy."

"It's their idea. Too many buckos loose with the same ambition you've got, but this outfit's clubby. So they change the room every night."

"Anyone I know?"

"Maybe. Bonal hits it once in a while when Hugh Mathias brings him. Then there's the super for the Pacific Shares, Herkenhoff. Curtin, the fire chief. Ferd Yates, the marshal. Sometimes, Chris Feldhake and——"

"Feldhake," Seay murmured, suddenly remembering Tober's mention of this man. "Do I know him?"

"He's a big blond moose and salty," Jimmy said. "You wouldn't forget him."

Seay shook his head. "Who else?"

"Well, one night Feldhake brought Janeece in. Bonal was there that night." He shook his head. "It was quite a party."

"Bonal won," Seay said.

"How'd you know?"

Seay only smiled and shifted in his chair. "Can I get in to-night?"

Jimmy studied him and then the canvas sack which lay on Seay's knee, and then he raised his glance again to meet Seay's eyes. "It can get pretty bloody, Phil."

"Sure. Can I get in?"

"Not if they're smart," Jimmy said dryly, rising. "Come on. They'll take my word for you."

They stepped out again into the mob in the bar-room. Jimmy shouldered his way to the back stairs and climbed them. At the top they travelled a long corridor to the rear of the building, then turned into another corridor at the right. These were the private rooms, where the girls below entertained their customers. At the end of this corridor, Jimmy stopped in front of a door and knocked on it, three sharp knocks, then one slight one. A muffled voice said, "Come in."

There was a big green-felted table in the centre of the large room, and the features of the five men seated around it were sharp and pale under the bright overhead lamp. Plainly this was a gambling room, formed by tearing out the partition and joining two rooms. A scarred sofa filled the back wall. There was a buffet beside it lined with a dozen bottles of liquor, glasses, a spacious tub of ice and three boxes of cigars. It was private, quiet, businesslike.

Jimmy spoke to the dealer, a small, white-haired man with shrivelled cheeks and oversize sabre moustaches.

"Ferd, you know Phil Seay."

"Sure," Yates said, nodding at Seay.

"Seay's looking for a game and some place to howl," Jimmy went on. "I told him I'd try for him here."

"If this is private, I don't want to," Seay murmured.

Yates looked at his companions. "Fresh money," he said, the corners of his eyes crinkling just a little to indicate he was smiling. He turned to Jimmy and Seay. "Ain't you the one Bonal broke the other night?" When Seay nodded, Yates said dryly, "Well, maybe this is somethin' I'm just a little better at than Charlie Bonal. Sure, sit in."

The others murmured assent, and Jimmy introduced Seay around. Yates, Curtin, Feldhake, House and Hugh Mathias were the names. Of them, Seay observed and noted two things, that Mathias wore immaculate clothes, and that Chris Feldhake could mangle a man's hand when he shook it.

Introductions finished, Jimmy said, "Start off, boys, and learn how to play stud from the man who invented it."

Seay took off his coat and sat down between Yates and Mathias, and while he bought his chips Mathias courteously explained the limit.

Soon the game was under way, and over this room came a feeling of concentrated reticence which is the universal atmosphere of gambling. When Seay backed out of three pots, Jimmy snorted in disgust, grinned and left.

Seay gambled with lazy attention, playing dull poker and studying everyone's hands but his own. It was Feldhake's hands that he studied most minutely, and how he played them. And slowly he got a knowledge of the man. Feldhake, at first sight, fitted only that part of Jimmy's description that called him a moose. Big he was, with a breadth of shoulder and thickness of neck that was massive, ponderous. His half-clenched fist could hide all his cards. At first sight, his face was pleasantly oafish, almost stupid, with its thick lips, bulbous nose and rough leathery skin. A permanent smile, uneasy almost, seemed stamped on the man's face. He smiled at everything and at everyone until a man watching him had the conviction that he thought the world a hugely pleasant place. That was a deception his eyes did not bear out, for they were deep-set, alert, wary, surface-lighted and opaque when a man looked squarely at them. A rough and untidy shock of blond hair, the slow speech of the man, the clumsy, bear-like movements of him seemed to give him an air of stupid simplicity. But it was quickly evident to Seay that Feldhake was gambling with a driving cunning and a card sense that was nearly intuitive. Mathias was the only other expert there. Yates, the quiet merchant, House, and the bluff and talkative Curtin were nonentities, playing for stakes that were too high for them.

Presently Seay leaned back and pulled out his watch and laid it beside him.

"I pull out at three," he said to the table. "That agreeable with you, gentlemen?"

They said it was. Seay won the next pot, and the one after that, which recouped a fifth of what he had lost. Slowly the game lost its air of feasty good-nature, with which most men gamble, and settled down in earnest.

At midnight Curtin lost his last chip and left, and Jimmy Hamp presently brought up a man named Trueblood to take his place. There was a swollen stack of chips in front of Seay. Jimmy chuckled at sight of them and said, "Boys, it costs a lot of money to learn poker the way he teaches it."

Feldhake laughed loudly at this. Jimmy went out and Trueblood bought his chips. At one Trueblood was losing badly and suggested to Feldhake they change seats. Feldhake agreed. In half an hour Trueblood was cleaned. His and Curtin's and House's chips were about evenly divided between Feldhake and Seay, who both had a sizeable share of Yates' and Mathias' too.

When Trueblood left, Feldhake rose and said, "Deal me out this round. I want a drink."

He went over to the buffet, poured a straight whisky and then walked to the window. He stood there, his great shoulders shoved through the window, breathing the hot but comparatively clean air, until Yates called wearily, "The deal's yours, Chris."

Feldhake pulled down the shade and returned to his seat.

At two-thirty, House and Mathias had lost half their chips to Seay and Feldhake, and Yates was playing a losing game in desperation. At quarter to three Yates threw down his cards, conceded the pot and rose to mix himself a drink.

"I never liked four-handed poker," Mathias observed.

"We've only got fifteen minutes of it," Seay countered, looking at Feldhake.

"Your luck's out, Mathias," House put in. "So's mine. Want to bank some blackjack?"

"Sorry, gentlemen, but that's not my game," Seay said. "I'll stay with it fifteen minutes."

Feldhake shrugged. "Pull out if you want."

Seay got a nod from Mathias and leaned back, stuffing his watch in his pocket. Yates returned with a drink and opened a cigar-box to cash in Seay's chips. The box was packed with banknotes.

"Paper," Yates said scornfully. "Where's it comin' from? Paper in a gold camp. Is it any good?"

They laughed at him. Paper money was a rarity in Tronah, and many workmen at the mines and mills would not accept it. Yates said to Seay, "You're the winner, Seay. You ought to take it."

Seay said he would, knowing he would have to get it changed in the morning. Seay rose then and left, just as the game was settling down to blackjack.

Out in the corridor he felt weary, this night's heat slugging at his temples with every beat of his heart. But in the canvas sack which he held loosely at his side was something over three thousand dollars in banknotes. In a smaller sack in his hip pocket was another thousand in gold pieces. The intolerable strain of knowing that for the last five hours he had been gambling with Charles Bonal's whole Tunnel scheme was gone now, and he felt drained of everything but the dregs of that vicious excitement.

Downstairs, the bar was less jammed, but it still held a thick crowd. He got a drink at the bar, then stepped out into the street. It, too, showed less people and less movement, and he turned down toward the feed corral, the heat of the night close and almost gagging.

A lantern hung in its arch. Tilted against the frame was an old man who roused from his doze as he heard Seay approach.

Seay flipped him a coin and said, "Sit tight, Dad," and tramped through the stables' long centreway to the corral in the rear. There had been a lantern hanging in the rear entrance when he put up his horse, but it was gone now, leaving the stable and its corral in darkness.

Once by the corral Seay turned and groped toward the hook on which the lantern hung.

He heard a sudden whisper of boots on the floor and wheeled, his hand driving toward his gun, and something crashed into the base of his skull.

Wave after wave of nausea coiled his stomach and he was fighting to his knees when he suddenly tried to open his eyes and found that he could.

First he saw the grained floor, dusted with wheat husks, and then he peered up into a lantern, held by the stable attendant. Reed Tober stood beside him, cursing in a bitter monotone.

Reed took his hand and hoisted him to his feet and then held his elbow while the room circled once and settled, and he shook his head.

"I got here too late," Tober said with quiet fury. "I got a shot, but it was a miss."

Seay raised a hand to the back of his neck and then brought it across his eyes and shook off Tober's hand.

"That was a sucker trick," he said mildly.

"They get it all?"

Seay reached in his hip pocket where the gold had been. It was empty. He nodded, and turned around to look for his hat. It lay over against a stall. Leaning to pick it up, he nearly fell, but he caught himself and then straightened and looked out into the street, his eyes narrowed. He shot one swift glance at the old man and opened his mouth to speak and then closed it.

"Come on," he said to Tober.

Tober fell in beside him. Seay's long stride took him upstreet.

Before they reached Jimmy Hamp's Keno Parlour, Seay paused and studied the second storey of the building. Then he turned and cut in between two buildings, whose narrow way was littered with trash.

Once in the alley, Seay turned up it and by the time Tober had caught up with him he had stopped again. He was looking at three lighted curtained windows, those of the gambling room he had just left.

"Give me all your matches," he said to Tober, and when he had them he walked up close to the building and struck a light. Tober watched him examine the ground in a wide circle, lighting a dozen matches in the process.

Then Seay came back and stood beside Tober and looked up at the window again. Tober heard his deep breathing.

"All right. Come along," Seay said quietly then.

They went into Jimmy Hamp's and up the stairs, turned the corridor angle. Before they reached the door of the gambling-room, Seay said, "This'll be rough, Reed. Don't let anyone surprise you from the corridor."

As he opened the door, Seay palmed up the gun and held it low, stepping in the room and aside for Tober to enter.

Mathias, Yates, House and Feldhake were still playing. They looked up at Seay and then they were motionless. Only Yates bothered to notice Tober's presence.

"Stand up, Feldhake," Seay said gently.

Tober drew his gun now, perhaps warned of what was coming, and without noticing him Seay rammed his own gun in his belt. Feldhake didn't move, and his uneasy smile didn't change.

"You played the wrong man for a Hiram this trip, Feldhake," Seay said. "It was pretty—only it was crude."

He glanced down at the stack of chips in front of Feldhake. "Cash his chips, Yates, and give me the money—four thousand."

Yates turned his head slowly, and when he was looking full at Feldhake, he said, "What is this, Chris?"

"Robbery, maybe," Feldhake said idly, softly.

"Two in twenty minutes then, Yates," Seay said, not looking at the marshal. "A couple of buckos knocked me over the head in the corral lot down street and took the money. It'll get back to Feldhake so I'll take it now."

"But——" Yates began, when Seay cut in, "Jimmy Hamp, marshal. First I thought Feldhake threw a note out the window, but it was Hamp that Feldhake got to. Cash those chips, Yates."

"But it could have been plain robbery," Yates said mildly.

"That was to-morrow's payroll for the tunnel crew," Seay murmured. "I don't know who told Feldhake we were short, but I'll find out. Cash those chips, Yates."

Feldhake said mildly, "You do, Ferd, and it's trouble."

Seay put a hand on Mathias' chair and wrenched it and Mathias was out of the way to let him stride over to Feldhake.

Feldhake was half risen, his hand brushing the skirt of his coat aside when Seay hit him, and he crashed over his chair to sprawl on the floor.

Seay followed him and stamped on the wrist of his hand that had hold of his gun, and when the gun fell he kicked it across the room.

Feldhake rose, lunging against the buffet, and he turned and grabbed a bottle by its neck, just as Seay crashed into him. The buffet went over and Feldhake, off balance, dropped the bottle to claw at the sofa arm, which braced him.

The impact of Seay's body against Feldhake made the lamp overhead dance, and Yates dodged aside. The sound of knuckle-studded fist on unpadded flesh smacked loud against an echoing grunt, and then the two men met, both upright, both slugging.

Each savage drive of Seay's fist caught Feldhake in the face, but it only served to keep him where he was, not to drive him back, and then Seay missed and they clinched. For five long seconds there was that gagging sound of indrawn breath as they wrestled, and then Feldhake heaved. When Seay crashed against the thin wall then, a window slammed down with a crack like the report of a gun.

Seay came in again, this time more quickly, lacing over long whipping blows that caromed off Feldhake's lowered head. Feldhake stumbled forward, his big arms flailing, and on the heel of bone-cracking uppercut from Seay, his head came up. Seay was to the side now, and the blow behind Feldhake's ear that was given so quickly Yates could not see was what sent Feldhake to the floor.

Seay was on him, and then under him, dragged by those

thick arms whose muscles ripped through the sleeve of Feldhake's shirt as they coiled and sawed and steadied. For a long moment they lay tied up side by side, and then slowly Seay's head went back under Feldhake's outspread palm, and then Feldhake's fist came down on Seay's jaw with the motion of a man stamping a letter with doubled fist. It gave Feldhake time to try and rise; but coming off the floor Seay caught him at his knees and rose, and in one terrific heave lifted him clear of the floor, shoulder high. Feldhake hung there for one dragging second, and then he crashed to the floor.

His breath went out in a cough and he tried to move, but Seay was astride him, pumping both fists into his face. Feldhake made a tentative, awkward move to rise, then lay back, quiet. Still Seay slugged at his face.

"That's enough, Phil," Tober said.

Obediently Seay stopped and rested both hands on Feldhake's chest, and dragged in great sobs of breath, head hung. The others waited, silent, until he looked up and then got unsteadily to his feet.

Somehow, the table had been shoved into a corner. The three blackjack hands lay undisturbed.

"The cash, Yates," Seay said, still panting.

Yates was regarding Feldhake, who had not moved. He shifted his gaze to Seay and said, "Is that straight? Did Jimmy Hamp put them on you?"

Seay nodded.

"All right," Yates said.

Hugh Mathias cleared his throat, and Yates counted out four thousand dollars, mostly in gold pieces, which he took out of the cigar-box in the overturned buffet.

He didn't say anything as Seay wheeled and went out the door. Tober closed it gently on these three men who were looking at each other, and then at the man on the floor.

Downstairs, Seay approached Jimmy Hamp's office and flung open the door, and Tober slid in before it swung shut.

Jimmy Hamp was having a drink with a man, and when the door opened he looked up at Seay. Slowly his face settled into slackness; only his eyes were wary and defeated.

Seay said, "It didn't work, Jimmy."

Jimmy looked at Tober and then, almost idly, he noted the torn clothes, the ribboned shirt, the ripped trousers of Seay. Presently he dragged his gaze up to Seay's face.

"No," he said quietly. "It didn't work." He put a soft hand

to his face and scoured his cheek with it, and said, " I'm sorry, Phil. I guess I don't have to tell you the rest."

Seay went out quietly, the anguish in his eyes as eloquent as that in Jimmy Hamp's, and Reed Tober closed the door without cursing.

Chapter V

After the women had left the room, Hugh Mathias signalled the waiter for more port. He accepted the box of cigars from the waiter and passed them around himself. Abe Comber belched and refused one, and while Blaine Mack and John Widows lighted up, Abe gnawed off a corner of a thin plug of tobacco and tucked the remainder in the pocket of his dress waistcoat. As the waiter leaned over his shoulder to pour his wine, Abe put a rough hand over his glass and said, " Bring me rye," and then regarded Hugh, who was lighting his own cigar before he sat down. Pleasant smoke filled this panelled lamp-lit room.

Abe Comber's seat was at the foot of the table, opposite Sharon, but now that she was gone the centre of attention seemed to devolve on him. It always did, for his rough backwoods frame and hard muscular face reflected a careless knowledge of power. If he had been only a mine manager, as these others here were, rather than the richest man on the Tronah Lode, he still would have commanded this room. And he achieved it by seeming to have a bull-headed disregard for things that were conventional and expected of him. Above all, he thoroughly enjoyed a total immunity from boredom; perhaps that was the secret of his power.

" Hugh," Abe began casually, breaking right into a conversation between Mack and Widows and silencing it, " I damn' near got in a fight to-day. Mighty, mighty close."

Hugh raised his eyebrows and waited for Abe to go on.

" A funny thing, too," Abe continued. " I didn't understand it rightly until it was too late." He tilted back in his chair. " Over you," he added.

" Over me?"

" Unh-huh. It was up in Judge Baily's law office. We were talking about the disappearance of three witnesses to a claim-jumping. Know anything about it?"

Hugh scowled and then laughed shortly. "I never saw a claim jumped in my life. Was I a witness?"

"No, Judge Baily went at it kind of back-handed. I claimed I wouldn't blame a witness for disappearing if he knew he'd only get in trouble by testifying. Baily claimed that it was his duty to testify, and that the safest thing to do was lay the information before the authorities and ask for protection. If he didn't do it, he was criminally negligible."

"What's that got to do with me?" Hugh inquired, frowning good-naturedly.

Abe regarded him with sober speculation. Mack and Widows were looking puzzled. "Nothing then. Only later, down at the Fifty-Two Club, it come to me that Baily was directly defaming you."

"But I never saw a claim jumped in my life," Hugh protested.

"This man at the club was talkin' about a poker game he'd heard about," Abe drawled. "He contends a properly staked claim was jumped—and with both feet." A trace of a smile played at the corners of Abe's wide mouth.

"In fact," Abe went on solemnly, "he claims you were one of the three four witnesses."

For a moment Hugh's face was plainly blank, and then something clicked and he took his cigar from his mouth and laughed. Abe laughed with him, leaving Mack and Widows completely in the dark.

"That," Hugh said, "is substantially correct. I refuse to testify."

"Then it did happen?" Abe asked.

Hugh inclined his head. "It did."

"How?"

Hugh tapped the ashes of his cigar into the tray and rose, looking down at Abe. "I learned something at that poker game, Abe. A man can have eyes and still can't see. It stood me so well that I still believe in it."

"But what happened?"

"You ask the other three witnesses." He tapped his shirt-front with his thumb. "I let the claim-jumpers talk first."

"You young whelp," Abe growled. "I talked to Yates."

Hugh had his watch out, looking at it, and he said to Abe as he put it back in his pocket, "Yates knows, Abe. He came awful close to getting his own claim jumped." He looked at Widows and Mack, and then again at Abe. "I'm sorry, but I've got an appointment to-night, so you'll have to excuse me."

They nodded, and Hugh turned to the door. Passing Abe, he laid a hand on Abe's shoulder and said, "Charles Bonal had the best hunch of his life there."

Abe grunted, chuckling quietly, and Hugh waved to the others and stepped out into the hall. He walked down it to the spacious living-room and opened the closet door to get his hat.

Sharon stepped out of an adjoining room, leaving the door ajar behind her. She crossed swiftly over to Hugh, who had his hat in his hand.

"Time to run, darling," he said.

Sharon's face didn't register Hugh's words. She put a hand on Hugh's arm and said, "Hugh, Maizie has been telling the most amazing thing about this man Seay. Is it true?"

"About the poker game? Yes."

"You were there and saw it," she said.

Hugh nodded, watching her face. "I was. Amazing hardly describes it."

"But why didn't you tell me?"

Hugh shrugged. "It's rather a personal matter of Seay's, I thought. I didn't blame him."

"Didn't blame him!" Sharon exclaimed.

"He was robbed. He seemed to know who robbed him and acted first and found out afterwards." He laughed shortly. "At any rate, the tunnel had pay-day Saturday. They tell me Seay's put up a yardage bonus and his crew is working like fury."

"But won't they do something to him?" Sharon exclaimed. "It was robbery of the worst kind."

Hugh shrugged.

"I think you admire him, Hugh!" Sharon accused.

"I do—in a way."

"After his insolence to me?"

Hugh patted her hand. "He meant it when he said he didn't have money. Besides, I still think you should have come to me."

"Perhaps I'll have to after this," Sharon said angrily. "After that telegram from Dad, I certainly don't intend to ask him for another dollar."

"It would be easier if you didn't."

Maizie came out of the adjoining room then with the wives of Mack and Widows. Maizie left them and came over to Hugh and Sharon.

"Is it true, Hugh, about this rip of a Seay?" Maizie demanded.

"Yes, Abe probably had the straight of it."

Maizie turned to Sharon. " Sharon, you're going to take me over to meet him to-morrow."

" I am not!" Sharon said hotly.

" Will you, Hugh?" Maizie asked.

Sharon said quickly, " If you do, Hugh, I'll be furious. A common tough!"

Hugh looked at Maizie and laughed. " I can't risk that, Maizie."

" All right," Maizie said grimly. " I'll go myself. I'm going to invite him to my party." She sniffed at Sharon and winked broadly. " Young woman, hard-bellied men like that are so scarce in this camp that I don't intend to stand on ceremony."

She turned and crossed the room, her silks swishing, to join the other two women, and Hugh and Sharon, arm in arm, went down the hall to the outside door.

" Maizie isn't funny at times," Sharon said quietly, and then laughed at herself. " She'll do just that, Hugh. You wait and see."

At the door Hugh said, " I'm sorry about having to leave, but it couldn't be avoided. You understand?"

Sharon patted his arm in understanding and then, anxiety on her face, she said, " Hugh, do you think Janeece wants to see you about—about tunnel business?"

" It's likely."

Sharon sighed. " Why, oh, why, does that man have to be such an octopus?"

" I've wondered," Hugh said quietly, grimly. " I don't like it either, Sharon. I'm heart and soul and body for your father, but at times like this my hands are tied." He looked down into her eyes. " I'm engineering a redistribution of stock, darling. Maybe when that's settled I can be a little more independent of him."

Sharon stood on tiptoe and kissed him, then closed the door softly. Hugh went below and through the lobby to the gig hitched just above the hotel, and while his driver handled the fretting horses through the crawling traffic, Hugh lighted a cigar and lounged back in the seat. A worried frown stamped his face, and he was suddenly and deeply disgusted with this camp. He threw away his cigar, and as they pulled out of the thick traffic of the streets and the horses stepped out, he regarded the night in moody silence.

The plant of the General Milling and Mining Company lay below town and to the south. It was one building, huge in proportions, and built in the shape of a Greek cross. The stamps of its mills boomed heavily into the night.

A quarter-mile from it they left the rutted freight road and took a smooth gravelled one. This approach to the mill was cared for, with iron lamp-posts spaced at regular intervals into the grounds. The mill building itself was a paradox. The north wing of it contained the offices, and fronting this wing was an artificial lake, around which the drive circled. In the middle of the lake was a fountain of cast bronze, Neptune with trident on an elaborate conch shell half smothered in waves. A wide border of precious grass edged the lake, and young shrubs edged the grass. This was Tronah, Hugh thought wearily, with so much free money that it lavished a pretty artificial lake on the ground of a stamp mill, the heaviest, most awesomely business-like industry of the whole camp. It was typical, for a tasteless ostentation was the mark of success here. Wasn't he driving a team of chestnuts from his suite in the Union house to his offices two miles away?—a thoroughbred team that was absurdly expensive and a monstrous care in this town where every bale of hay, every measure of oats, must be freighted over two mountain ranges. Didn't he have champagne with lunch, followed by a three-dollar cigar which the dry air had already ruined?

Tronah was no city; it was desert, but it was more profligate with money than any city since Rome. And with plain dirt miners, freighters, cheap gamblers, and storekeepers for its peerage, its taste was that of a brothel. It bred strong men only to mock them with their own vulgar actions. Money bought anything, except a few women like Sharon. And strangely, Hugh considered, he was wanting money so he could have her. Right now he had a tiny toehold in the big feed trough of Bonanza, and with luck and a little shrewdness, he would end up with both feet in it. If Janeece willed it. The thought of the man curdled Hugh's disgust. It wasn't the fact that this man, also self-made, had all the power of the west coast banks concentrated in his frail hands that angered him; it was the fact that with him, Charles Bonal's enemy, Hugh was almost sure to cast his lot.

He said curtly, "Stop," as they reached the massive iron gates in front of the office, and he alighted from the gig.

"Wait for me here," he added.

He walked slowly around the lake, feeling its almost cool emanation. One section of the north wing had lights in the windows, and he knew Janeece was inside. Conquering his reluctance, he approached the entrance.

The night watchman at the big door said, "Evening, sir," and held the door open. Hugh walked down the softly lighted, more softly carpeted corridor, a rank of inscribed doors on his right. Beyond the corridor the great stamps were thundering, and the building vibrated lightly under his feet. Back there men were working like demons, the smell of sweat and steam and acid and hot ore in their noses, the crashing of the huge stamps rocking the air to heavy bedlam. Here, only the faint perfume of expensive cigars seduced the senses—and this was the more savage part of the whole.

He entered Janeece's waiting-room without knocking. The door to the inner office was open, and Hugh put his hat on a chair and walked to the door and knocked softly.

He was bid enter, and he stepped inside, closing the door behind him. This was a rich room, its leaded windows opening out on to a view of the lake. An ornate crystal lamp sat at one corner of the huge desk by the window; Servel Janeece, a frail ghost, sat on the other corner.

"Hallo, Hugh." Janeece waved a hand towards a humidor on the desk and said, "This is inconvenient, I'm afraid."

"Not at all, sir," Hugh said quietly. He took a cigar and sat down in one of the deep leather chairs and did not light his cigar immediately, but watched Janeece.

He wondered idly if Janeece was consumptive, and then immediately he remembered that he had asked himself that same thing before, and that he had never heard him cough. The pallor of the man's face was almost luminous, heightened by dead black clothes and loosely knotted black tie. Janeece was a small man and he had a small tired voice, but his was not the small man's way, for it was the opposite of aggressive. He was utterly reasonable, quietly and apologetically logical, and ruthless as death. His dark eyes always held a sardonic reserve which he never voiced. Playing men and money one against the other apparently gave him little pleasure. Hugh did not know what drove him, nor did he know a man who could tell him. Janeece, of course, never would.

"Dinner at the Bonals'?" Janeece inquired, and when Hugh nodded, he added, "A lovely girl, with most of Bonal's qualities."

"His good ones?" Hugh murmured.

Janeece laughed. "Most of his are good, Hugh. It just happens he's made the mistake of wanting too much."

Hugh said nothing, but let the peace of the room hold him.

"I understand you were a party in the poker game the other night which has already become famous," Janeece said, his smile gentle, his eyes speculative.

"A crude trick," Hugh said. "I'm surprised it would be resorted to."

"You put that nicely," Janeece said, and laughed. "It happens it was an idea of Chris's, not mine."

"I could tell that. Robbery seldom has a finesse unless it's pulled by a good stage robber or a better banker."

Janeece smiled to himself and went around his desk and sat down. "You're a little sharp to-night, Hugh."

"I don't like what I'm going to hear," Huge replied frankly.

Janeece said, "Doubtless." He was silent a moment, looking out the window. "I have information," he began slowly, "that Charles Bonal did not get on the boat that was to take him to Mexico." He looked lazily at his thin hands. "Either he's in no hurry, or he's not going to Mexico City."

"It won't make much difference if he gets there or not, will it?"

Janeece still looked at his hands. "No. How did you know that?"

"I guessed it. You've probably arranged to destroy his reputation and credit there long since," Hugh said.

"Of course." He paused. "I wish I knew where he was."

"I can't tell you," Hugh said. "I wouldn't if I could." He smiled faintly. "I'm for giving him a fighting chance, anyway."

"You won't be in a position to," Janeece murmured.

Hugh sighed. "All right. Let's hear it."

"I want you to call in your loans to Bonal," Janeece said idly. "There's a chance in a million he'll be in with more money soon. I'm going to start turning the screw."

"Afraid of Seay?"

"He's a man with imagination. Why not be careful?"

"I could put up a scrap about this," Hugh said presently.

"You won't though," Janeece replied. He looked out the window again. "I'm in a position to trade with you."

"What could you give me that would be worth what I'm giving you?"

"Money."

Hugh flushed. "How much?"

"As much as you can turn it into," Janeece answered.

"To-morrow my agents in San Francisco can start dumping Dry Sierras Consolidated stock—reason unnamed. My men are pretty shrewd guessers," he added. "People follow them."

Hugh was attentive.

"I have enough of your stock—or I can get enough—that it will look serious. It will start a considerable market flurry." He shifted his gaze to Hugh now. "I'll lend you the money to buy all of it that your men can pick up for you."

Hugh laughed uncomfortably. "Which is just another way of buying Consolidated stock for yourself, seeing as you'll have my note for the money loaned."

"No. That note will never be collected if you're willing to go all the way with me. You can have your own lawyer write the ticket, so it'll be airtight. If you come through for me when I really need you—and I think you know when that will be—then we'll cancel my loan. You'll have undisputed control of the Dry Sierras Consolidated, then." He waited a moment and then added, "Isn't that a fair trade?"

Hugh was silent a long moment, and Janeece didn't bother to observe him. Presently Hugh said, "You know, Janeece, I wonder at you. Surely you know these mines can't go much deeper without Bonal's tunnel. If I got control of the Dry Sierras it would be a pity that it turned *borrasca* because it was filled with the water Charles Bonal could have drained from it."

Janeece said, "There are pumps."

"Big enough to care for another five hundred feet of water. What then?"

"Others will be invented. When we first hit water there wasn't a pump made that could lift it high enough. One was invented. The same thing will happen again."

"You forget gravity," Hugh murmured.

"The engineers have never let it stop them."

Hugh was silent. Slowly Janeece turned his chair and put both elbows on the desk. "You're sure of another five hundred feet of ore free of water, Hugh. I've got pretty accurate information that your veins are widening and that in another two months you'll almost double your take. Is that right?"

Hugh inclined his head.

"All right. You'll be in control before you have gone another hundred feet deeper." Janeece spread his hands. "That will leave you another four hundred feet of Bonanza. With this stock you'll acquire, that's enough to make you a rich man.

When pumps are developed that can pump water from another five hundred feet lower, you'll be a very rich man."

"But will they?" Hugh asked insistently.

Janeece put both hands on his desk. "They will, Hugh. I tell you, that mine and all its wealth will be yours. I'm handing it to you in return for your co-operation." He raised a thin finger then. "Mind, it's not my belief that Bonal can put that tunnel through. It can't be done—not without money even, and I've seen to it that he can't get that. But if—'if' I said—the tunnel, by some wild chance, will be put through, then I'll need your help. And I pay for the help I get. That's why I'm doing this for you."

Hugh finally lighted his cigar. The two men sat in comfortable silence long enough to let Hugh finish his smoke. The quiet had grown enormous, so that every movement of the stamps back in the mill seemed magnified a hundred times.

Hugh rose. "All right. Give me time to put my agents in San Francisco on the job."

"I knew you'd see it that way," Janeece said quietly. "I'll never need to resort to your help to break Bonal, for the tunnel will never go through. But if I do need to, you won't fail me, Hugh."

Hugh understood the innuendo, and he smiled wryly. "Hardly. You've seen to that."

"Haven't I?" Janeece murmured. He stood up and put out his hand.

"Good-night, Hugh. You've made a wise decision."

Chapter VI

Borg Hulteen, the shift boss and head driller, looked suspiciously at the new timbering and mopped the water out of his eyes. It was staunch, of ten-by-ten pine beams, and it tightly sealed the roof and walls of the tunnel for a space of forty feet. Borg glanced over at Seay, who was naked to the waist too, his body smeared with dirt and runnelled with sweat, his mouth open to get all the good out of this hot and fetid and stinking air.

The drill crew and the muckers stood in a loose circle eyeing the work, then glanced at the pile of rock and rubble which almost blocked the tunnel and which an hour before had thundered down to the tunnel floor, leaving a gaping hole in the tunnel roof. The small slide had dammed the floor of the tunnel, so that the water which ran beside the double tracks had backed up to the drill some fifty feet away at the tunnel-head.

Seay felt the water around his knees warm and viscous with mud. Five Cornish timbermen, their tools still in their hands, squinted up in the steaming lantern light at their work.

"All right, you bloody limeys," Borg growled. "Is it safe?"

The Cornishmen nodded, and Borg glanced over at Seay. "All right?"

"Put off a shot and we'll see," Seay told him. The muckers shovelled away the rock and rubble from the track, and a dump car was brought up to the drill. The flexible hose from the drill to the receiving tank down the tunnel was uncoupled, the drill loaded on the dump car, and the dump car hauled back away from the tunnel-head.

Seay and Borg placed the dynamite, lighted the fuses, and went back where the muckers and the Cornishmen were waiting. Soon the explosion boomed through the tunnel, and they went forward again. The timbers had held easily; only a faint rattle of rock on them indicated that any dirt and rock in the fault had been displaced by the vibration.

Borg Hulteen turned to the muckers and said, "Get busy, boys. Move it." He looked over at Seay. For an hour now they had been working furiously, getting the timbers up, their thoughts on only one thing, to check the slide before it poured half the mountain into the tunnel. Now, looking at Seay, Borg's homely Scandinavian face lost some of its tenseness.

"I don't like that," he said fervently.

"That was your mistake, Borg," Seay said. "You should have spotted that and timbered it."

Borg nodded wearily. "That's right."

"No alibi?" Seay asked sharply.

Borg shook his head, and only then did Seay smile. This head driller was a big raw-boned man with the pale flesh of a man who works out of sunlight. But his eyes were rimmed with sleeplessness and his every movement was weary.

"The devil you haven't," Seay said quietly and in complete friendliness. "You're coming off at noon, Borg, and get twelve hours' sleep. To-morrow you'll drop the midnight shift to Lueter. If he can stand the heat, you'll divide the shifts."

"That damn' square-head," Borg said contemptuously. "You want to order a half-dozen new drills? Last night

McCarty caught him with the drill so far back from the face that the piston'd of kicked the end out of the cylinder. Why, he don't——"

"You do what I say," Seay said grimly. "When you get so woolly you'll pass something like that, you're not safe, Borg."

Borg swore now, but he was grinning. "I didn't mean it, Phil. Lueter's all right—only, damn the slowness of him! He's an old woman."

Seay jerked his head towards the crew. "Get this muck cleared out of here and come off at noon."

Draggingly, Seay turned down the tunnel. A short way down it two mules were standing, hitched to a string of empty dump cars, the lanterns on their collars burning steadily in this semi-gloom. Soon they would be hauling the filled cars out, while other teams dragged empties in, making the line never-ending. A half-naked driver was sitting on one of the cars, and Seay nodded to him as he passed.

Presently, after minutes of walking, he heard the mules coming down with the filled cars. He waited, and swung up beside the driver and rode the rest of the way out of the tunnel.

At the mouth, Seay hopped off, squinting against the blinding glare of the sun. Scrubbing the sweat and dirt from his body with the wet shirt, he tramped down the slope towards the buildings, the water squishing in his boots. The rest on the car had made him less tired, but he did not think of that. Mentally he was calculating when the upcast, which was being dug on the slope above, would meet the tunnel. No reasonable man would have asked this tunnel crew to work in that heat and that danger, and it angered Seay that they had to. Tonight the pipe-line would be put through to the head of the tunnel, and a cool stream of water would be running continually for the men to bathe in and drink. That would help a little until they got the upcast completed and the blowers in.

He walked head down, scowling, his shirt wadded in his fist, the sun hammering on his bare back. A workman spoke to him and Seay did not hear him.

When he crossed a patch of shade, thrown by the long bunkhouse, he looked up and around him. Down in front of the office a team and brougham were stopped. Someone after Bonal, he thought, and possibly a creditor. The back of the brougham hid the occupants, to whom Tober, foot on the wheel hub, was talking.

"Phil," Tober called, and Seay cut over to them. As he

approached, Tober stepped away, and Seay looked squarely at Sharon Bonal. There was an older woman beside her, and for a second Seay's face hardened. He remembered then that he was half-naked, fouled with mud and sweat, but it gave him a perverse pleasure to see the colour mount to Sharon Bonal's face as she looked at him and then away. Tober stifled a smile and touched his hat and walked away.

"Good-morning," Sharon stammered faintly. Ben, looking down from the driver's seat at Seay, grinned and addressed his attention to the horses.

"Mrs. Comber, this is Mr. Seay," Sharon said coldly.

Maizie leaned forward to look at Seay across Sharon. Her survey was shrewd, friendly, slow.

"Your hands are dirty, and I'm glad they are," she said, extending her hand. "It's the first dirty hand I've shaken in too long a time."

Seay took her hand, the reticence in his long face thawing out a little. When he saw the friendliness of her eyes he almost smiled. "It's dirty all right, Mrs. Comber."

"Mrs. Comber wants to see the tunnel," Sharon said rapidly. "I'm sure it will be all right if I wait here while you take her through."

Seay's glance shifted to her and she saw the insolence come into his grey eyes. The long muscles of his arms moved a little as he lifted his arm to place a hand on his knee. There was no shame in the man, she thought hotly, but still she looked at the thick shoulders capped by deep ropes of muscle. Seay was staring at her thoughtfully.

"That's nice," he drawled coolly. "Maybe you'd like me to call the drill crew out so Mrs. Comber could go in there the only way anybody can stand it—half-naked."

Sharon stifled a gasp. Maizie only chuckled and looked sharply at Sharon. "You little liar," she said amiably. "I don't want to see the tunnel." Then she contradicted herself. "Yes I do. I'd love to see it. Only I'm an old woman and I loathe heat, and I'm not spry enough to run around half-naked a mile into the ground."

Sharon blushed hotly now, and Seay looked swiftly at Maizie. Then he laughed softly, and Sharon shot him a swift glance of venomous dislike.

"What I came out for was to extend an invitation that'll probably be refused," Maizie said. When Seay didn't reply, she went on. "Adelina Patti is singing at the opera house Saturday night. Afterwards, I'm having a reception for her at my house. I want you to come—and I mean it when I say I *want* you to."

Seay studied Maizie's face with reflective eyes, and then he turned his head to look away.

Maizie went on placidly. "Nothing in the world can make Abe Comber wear a boiled shirt. I'm giving this party mainly because it's expected of me, not because I like to. I'll have a dull time. If I could get more like you, young man, I would have a good time." She settled back in her seat and said firmly, "You'll come, even if Sharon thinks you won't."

Seay said casually to Maizie, and Maizie only, "Even if I have to drink rye whisky?"

Maizie looked quickly at him and then at Sharon, who was kneading a fold of her pale lawn dress. Maizie opened her mouth to speak and then she lay back against the cushions and laughed. Seay's face was perfectly sober, but there were small dancing lights in his eyes.

He stepped away and said, "If I'm free, I'll come, Mrs. Comber. Thank you."

Maizie waved to Ben to drive on, and Ben whipped up the horses. Sharon's face was turned towards Ben's back and was rigid with humiliation as they drove off. Seay stood there a moment, watching the brougham, and on his face was the look of an impudent boy. Turning, he tramped across to the office, whistling thinly.

That night at the mess-table Seay finished supper first. As he reached for his pipe, Tober glanced obliquely at him and then continued eating. Seay regarded each man at the table. Only Kelly was absent, for he was personally bossing the laying of the water-pipe. The heat of this small room was stifling. Tilting back in his chair, Seay filled his pipe and rammed his pouch in his pocket. He was studying these men in a curious, unhostile way, yet they were aware of it all the time.

"Reed, you and Cruickshank and Hardiston step down to the office after supper. And ask Kelly for the dump-car count for the first three hours of Lueter's shift."

He rose and went out, and after he was gone the atmosphere was a little freer. Down at the office he lighted the lamp and sat down in the swivel-chair and hoisted his feet to the desk. The single window was open, and a hot wind rode through the room, ruffling the untidy heap of papers on his desk-top. He smoked and stared at the wall, listening for a sound. When he got it—that of men approaching the shack—he did not move.

Cruickshank entered first, his heavy boots booming on the

hollow floor. Seay pointed with a pipe to the chairs and said, "Sit down," and watched Cruickshank's slow, deliberate movements as he hauled up three chairs. Cruickshank was a rough and untidy man with a powerful frame that had slacked off to fat, and kind of sour scowl on his pale face. He was a man of action, chained to a desk and draughting table by a keen knowledge of a job he did not like, and Seay understood that this was why he drank too much. He shifted his attention to Hardiston, the spare and precise little book-keeper whom Charles Bonal had carried around with him, like a pair of comfortable slippers, for some twenty years. In that small skull, with its saddle of grey hair from ear to ear, there was vast and thorough knowledge of Bonal's business, Seay knew. Hardiston turned to get a match from Reed and then seated himself, puffing carefully on his cigar, after he lit it, to even the ash. He had the sturdy obsequiousness of the indispensable underling. He was right all the time, and he knew it and seemed content.

Cruickshank sprawled his feet out and said, "You think Lueter will do for two shifts?"

"I think he's got to," Seay murmured. Reed leaned against the wall, watchful.

Seay sucked on his cold pipe, then hunched forward and laid it on the desk, asking, "You satisfied with your wages, you three?" and turned to regard them.

Cruickshank spoke up immediately. "No."

Seay shifted his gaze to Hardiston, and Hardiston said carefully, "Not exactly. Under the circumstances, however, it's enough."

Seay didn't have to look at Reed, who said, "Yes," whereupon Seay tilted back in the chair.

He began slowly. "You three—we four, I should say—are the only persons who have access to the tunnel books, besides Charles Bonal, aren't we?"

"Yes," Hardiston said.

"You, Cruickshank, because you've got to run for the balance sheet every time a drill breaks," Seay said. Cruickshank nodded meagrely. "And you, Hardiston, because it's your business as book-keeper and paymaster. Reed knows it for the same reason I do, because he wonders every week how we'll pay off the men."

He waited a moment before he continued, and he could see nothing but idle curiosity in these three. Reed's face, he couldn't see at all, and he didn't want to.

"You're sure?" he asked slowly. "You're sure nobody else can get at these books?"

"They're in the safe," Cruickshank said bluntly. "How could anyone else?"

Seay said, "They couldn't." He paused. "One of us four here has sold to outsiders—to Janeece and to Feldhake, specifically—information contained in our books. I gambled with tunnel funds last Friday night in a poker game. Somebody gave out the information that we had less than two thousand dollars to meet the pay-roll with. I showed up with that two thousand at that poker game and was later robbed of it and my winnings in gold pieces." He added mildly, "I don't suppose any of you care to admit it now."

There was a long and uncomfortable silence, then Cruickshank snorted. "Who the hell would admit if he had?"

"Someone will," Seay said gently.

"That's one hell of a charge," Cruickshank said idly.

"Speaking of charges, what right had you to gamble with tunnel funds?" Hardiston asked.

"None."

"Are you going to tell Mr. Bonal?"

"I am. Or you can, Hardiston."

Hardiston shrugged. "I'm merely pointing out that you aren't free of blame yourself."

Seay nodded quietly, and looked up at Reed. Reed's gaze held his.

"That's all," Seay said finally. "I'll know the traitor soon—if he doesn't skip out. Good-night, gentlemen."

Cruickshank and Hardiston went out, but Tober remained. Seay filled his pipe again and lighted it, and said, "Which one—Reed?"

"I don't know," Tober said, lounging erect from the wall and walking over to the window. He stood with his hands rammed in his pockets, looking out at the rank of hulking buildings in the night, and presently murmured, "You're a hard man, Phil."

"I want loyalty," Seay said vehemently. "Bonal deserves it. I do. Any man worth his food deserves it!"

Tober half-turned from the window to regard Seay's back.

"You don't get it by asking for it."

Seay swivelled his head to look at him. "I get it by demanding it."

Tober walked across to the door, and before he went out he

paused beside the desk. "Damned if you don't," he said, and left.

For three days Seay left Cruickshank and Hardiston alone. Two nights he worked one of Lueter's shifts himself, until, slowly, the German shift boss could learn to bear the heat of the tunnel. Tober wanted to spell him, but Seay would not allow it. And ponderously, with the steady fury of obsession, the tunnel went deeper and deeper into the Pintwater.

It was after one of these shifts, at six o'clock in the morning, that Seay came out of the tunnel. The denim trousers and wooden-soled boots he wore were dripping water. He was clean, having bathed under the cold-water pipe before he left the tunnel-head, and he went directly to the mess-hall. Breakfast and a clean shirt were set out for him, and he slumped into the chair, too tired to eat immediately.

Half-way through breakfast he heard someone approach, and Hardiston stepped inside. Never in all this heat had Hardiston been seen without a coat, and he wore it now, even though the comparative cool of early morning was already being blotted up by the sun.

Seay greeted him. "You're up early, Hardiston."

Hardiston took the bench opposite. "It's the only time I can see you alone. I—I've been a while making up my mind about this."

Seay continued eating, occasionally covertly observing Hardiston. If the man wanted to talk, Seay intended to hear him, but he would not help him.

"It's about this matter you spoke of the other night," Hardiston said.

"All right."

"I don't like to do this, only the way you've put it up to us, it's a case of simple survival."

Seay kept silent.

"Bonal has trusted me for twenty years," Hardiston said.

Seay glanced up at him. "Why shouldn't he?"

"I don't mean that. I mean I've minded my business and known my job. I learned that in New England."

Still Seay did not help him.

"This isn't minding my business," Hardiston went on, urgency in his eyes. "I want you to understand it's distinctly disagreeable—against every principle I have."

To which Seay nodded gravely.

"It's about Tober."

"Go on."

The little man started to speak, and then cleared his throat and began again. "The way I understand it, you were robbed at McGrew's stable, weren't you? There was no lantern at the corral, and in the dark there someone slugged you and robbed you of your gold."

"That's right."

"Tober was standing beside you when you regained consciousness. Isn't that queer?"

"What's queer about it?" Seay asked swiftly.

"Why didn't he join you at Hamp's?"

Seay carefully laid down his knife and fork and said, "Come out with it, man! Are you saying Tober robbed me?"

Hardiston shrugged his slim shoulders and, unsmilingly, said, "That isn't all. I haven't got proof for what I'm about to say."

"You haven't got proof for what you've already said."

Doggedly Hardiston reminded Seay that each morning it was his duty to stop at the express office to sign bills of lading on out-going freight and to see if the tunnel teams were to call for freight. On Saturday morning, Hardiston said, he'd stepped behind the express office wicket to check some off-size drills, which were being returned to the makers in San Francisco. "While I was counting them," he went on carefully, "I noticed a small package addressed in the same handwriting as the drill tags."

"Tober's handwriting, you mean."

"Yes. I thought the package was one of the drill collars Tober was returning."

"What changed your mind?"

"When I picked it up, it clinked, like a box of assorted washers."

The two men stared at each other a long moment, Hardiston's gaze unfaltering. Presently Seay said:

"Are you trying to tell me this package held gold coins?"

"I'm not trying to tell you anything. I'm relating what happened."

"Remember the address?"

"No. Except that it wasn't Murray's, where the drills were going." He hesitated. "Why should I? I thought finally it was a personal package of Tober's."

Seay said, "That's pretty thin proof."

"I said it wasn't proof."

Seay kicked the bench away from him and walked over to the door, his face dark. Hardiston watched him without rising.

"You think this package weighed enough to——?" Seay paused and began again. "Would four thousand in gold pieces weigh the same as this package?"

"That's one thing I can answer," Hardiston said firmly. "I haven't been a paymaster for nothing. The answer is definitely yes."

"You think it was gold?"

"That's for you to answer."

Seay said carefully, "Thanks, Hardiston. I won't go to Tober with it. I realise it's only a hunch, maybe a valuable one."

Hardiston joined him at the door. "That's off my mind," he said firmly. "I don't accuse anyone. On the other hand, I want my name cleared."

Together they left the mess-hall and walked as far as the bunk-house, where they parted. In three minutes Seay was in his bunk and asleep.

It was almost noon when Tober shook him, and it was like trying to fight off a drug to come awake. Tober swung his legs to the floor and held him in a sitting position until Seay raised his head.

"Bonal's here," Tober said, excitement in his voice.

Seay heard that and he shook his head, muttering, "Bonal?"

"Yes. Want to see him?"

"I'll get my clothes on."

Charles Bonal was sitting in the swivel-chair when Seay entered a few moments later. Reed Tober was smiling as Bonal rose and shook Seay's hand. Hardiston and Cruickshank were in the room, and the five men chatted together for a few minutes, after which Cruickshank and Hardiston left.

Bonal settled back in his chair and passed cigars to Seay and Tober.

"Mexico City must have moved north considerable since I last saw it," Seay observed.

"I didn't go to Mexico City and never intended to," Bonal chuckled. He pointed to his beard, which was clipped and combed neatly. His eyes were less pouched, almost fresh, and he smoked his cigar with slow relish. "Can't you guess where I've been?"

"San Francisco."

Bonal inclined his head. "That Mexico City trip was a

blind. Janeece has men down there now, scuttling my ship." He smoked thoughtfully. "I did my business in a cheap hotel, and with Mexican mine-owners from San Luis Potosi, who were in town at my request."

"Good God, Bonal," Tober blurted out. "What did you find out? That's what we want to hear!"

Bonal deliberately waited a moment while he carefully flicked the ash from his cigar. "We have money," he announced then. "Not an awful lot, but if we handle it carefully, it'll do us."

Tober said pardonably, "Jesus!" and sighed.

"The stage-driver on the Walker River-Tronah leg assured me last night that the tunnel was still running," Bonal murmured, observing Seay. "He also mentioned something about a poker game."

Tober said dryly, "Liars, those stage-drivers, to a man."

Bonal rose and peeled off his coat, still avoiding Seay's eyes. Then he yanked off his tie and said to no one in particular, "I think, gentlemen, that all three of us can stand considerable kicking around." His gaze touched Seay, and for a moment it held all of a grateful man's thanks. "Let's look at the tunnel."

The three of them went out, but Seay paused in the outer office and said to Hardiston, "Come with me a moment, Hardiston."

Outside, and away from the door, they faced each other. Tober and Bonal, in shirt-sleeves, were deep in conversation as they walked past the bunk-house. The sun hammered mercilessly from overhead, causing Hardiston to squint as he looked up at Seay's cold and impassive face.

"Bonal came back too soon for me to spare you all of it, Hardiston. If I were you, I'd pack up now, while Bonal is in the tunnel. You won't have to face him if you hurry."

"Pack up?" Hardiston murmured, watching Seay's face with unblinking eyes.

"Yes, you see, that money I was robbed of was mostly in bank-notes, not gold. That's the trap I laid. Tober couldn't have changed the notes, because he was with me till daylight. He didn't address the package, or take it to the express office."

For a long moment Hardiston regarded him, his neatly shaven face unexpressive. "He could have addressed it the night before and his confederates could have expressed it."

"Man," Seay said with tolerant patience, "I'm only trying to keep you from facing Bonal for it. Take your choice."

"I'll go," Hardiston said finally. "Thank you, Seay."

Seay walked off. He paused in mid-stride and came back to Hardiston, who was standing motionless. "Why did you do it?" Seay asked, his voice kindly.

"For a lot of money," Hardiston murmured, and walked off towards the office.

Chapter VII

Stoles Opera House, a bravely painted board affair of some three storeys and a gingerbread front, witnessed immortality that night. To a gold camp, starved for music and ignorant of her technique, Adelina Patti sang for two hours. It was all in good humour, but these rough miners who jammed the house from pit to gallery would not let her go. If her reluctance to sing encores was known to them, as it was to the theatre of New York and Chicago, they ignored it and called her back. Time and again she stood and stamped her foot in refusal to sing again, and time and again they made her. Her dark, chiselled beauty was like a wine of her own Latin countries, fiery and proud, and these rough men hungered for a sight of it and for her voice. At last she gave in and sang for another hour, and perhaps because it was in waltz time, they shook the building with their applause for her "*Fior de primavera,*" not a word of which they understood. When it came to time for her "Home, Sweet Home," which countless times had thrilled less sentimental audiences than this, its lyric message was so moving that pandemonium was let loose. The miners howled down Dan Stole each of the twenty-five times he appeared in front of the curtain to tell them Patti had left. A group of tearful Italian miners in the front row made the first considerate move to go. They were jeered wildly, but it served to break up the evening, and reluctantly the house started to empty.

Sharon and Hugh and Charles Bonal walked the few doors from the opera house to the hotel, and went upstairs.

Sharon was first into the room, and as she stepped over the sill she stopped abruptly. Phil Seay stood before the chair he had just risen from, his pipe in his hand, looking taller than usual in his black clothes.

Charles Bonal said over Sharon's shoulder, "Been here long, Phil?" and Sharon stepped reluctantly into the room.

"A few minutes."

All three were in the room now, and Charles Bonal turned to Hugh. " I believe you two have met," he said dryly.

Hugh laughed and put his hand out to Seay. " I believe we have, although the meeting wasn't official."

Seay said, " How are you, Mathias?"

" Considerably more at ease than when I last left you."

Bonal was laughing at this as Sharon swept past them down the hall. Bonal caught the maid before she disappeared, and said, " Bring whisky and ice, Sarita." To Hugh and Seay he said, " Sit down. I'll be with you in a moment, Phil," and he followed Sharon. She was waiting at the door of her room, and she beckoned him in and closed the door, and said vehemently, " Dad, he's not going with us!"

" Who said he was?" Bonal showed surprise.

" But why is he here?"

" I asked him." He grinned into his beard, then laughed bluntly at his daughter. She had barely mentioned to him Seay's refusal to give her money for Maizie, but he guessed how her pride had suffered. Always unable to refuse her anything himself, he delighted to see another man tame her, for he was not completely blind to the fact that Sharon must learn some day that other people besides herself possessed a will. Hugh was not much help in this department. Right now Bonal could not precisely understand her agitation. Her face had lost some of the calm loveliness it had when she was listening to Patti, and there was quite genuine anger in her eyes. Inside the fragile white beauty of her dress, her slim body was taut. Bonal took her hands now, and his face sobered.

" Here, child," he said gruffly. " Can't a man ask his own friends up for a drink before a party?"

" I suppose." Sharon's voice was nicely controlled.

" If you can't tolerate him, I won't ask him any more. Tonight I wanted to give you two young folks some time to yourself," he said more gently. " Seay was going out to Maizie's, and I thought I'd take him. Besides that, I like him."

" I don't. He's "—she was going to say " insulting," but she knew it would anger her father into demanding definite proof, and the proof she gave him would make him roar with his rough laughter.

" He's what?"

" He's not a gentleman!"

" No, thank the Lord," Bonal sighed. " He's a man, though, and that's something much rarer. He's a man who can't be licked."

"But, Dad, you picked him up off the streets!" Sharon protested. "You put a lot of faith in character. Do you know his?"

"Better than I know Hugh's," Bonal replied quickly, "and that's no reflection on Hugh."

"But a gambler, a tough!"

"I recollect I was a swamper in a St. Louis bar-room once," Bonal said dryly. "I even banked faro—and worse than Seay did."

Sharon dropped her gaze and walked away from him. Bonal's face was vaguely troubled as he raised his hand to the door-knob. "He won't bother you, my dear." Tentatively he made his suggestion. "Have you ever tried treating him with less of a high hand?"

Sharon whirled, her skirts billowing, but when she saw that her father was serious, she choked down her protest and considered. "No, I hadn't. I really didn't ever dream I'd be forced to associate with him."

"And why wouldn't you associate with him?" Bonal asked testily.

"I don't know. All your superintendents before this were—were not our sort of people. Oh, I don't mean they weren't all right, but we didn't entertain them. They were like workmen."

Bonal winced inwardly, but he only said, "Aren't his manners all right?"

"When he wants them to be."

"Doesn't he dress right?"

Sharon nodded. "I thought he looked remarkably handsome to-night," she said frankly.

"That's better," Bonal said quietly. "He's presentable, in other words. And now the only complaints outstanding are that you dislike him and that he's a workman, which he is. The first is your own business. The second is snobbishness. So"—he smiled again—"I can't respect your judgment in this case." He opened the door and winked at her. "The Old Man has spoken—and as usual, to deaf ears."

Sharon made a face at him and then laughed, and they were both in good humour as he left. In his own room he changed his shoes, wondering at the ways of his daughter, rose from the bed and walked over to a box of cigars which lay open on the table. Reluctantly he emptied his breast coat-pocket of a rank of black, squat cigars, and filled it again with these slim, light-coloured ones from the box—his lone concession to mixed company. He got a soft hat and went out to the parlour, where Seay and Hugh were talking. He took Seay and went out.

Comber's house, seen from the ridge, was a blaze of lights in all three storeys. A great rank of carriages almost blocked the drive, for this was one of the Comber parties, and not to be treated lightly.

Ben, sheepish in an emergency butler's uniform, took their hats in the foyer, and the solemn wink that Seay gave him was a slight compensation for the indignity of trading a stable full of quiet horses for a house full of noisy people.

Maizie and Abe Comber were receiving in the huge doorway, in the rooms beyond which most of the guests were assembled. Maizie was wearing a dress of rich purple silk, and on her ample bosom was a huge diamond pendant that almost vied with the brilliance of the crystal chandelier behind her. The hand she extended to Seay was so beringed that it felt like a handful of metal. She said, " You go on in and get a drink. You'll need it."

Abe, true to Maizie's prediction, was wearing a soft unpleated shirt, and he eyed them and the company with a mild and expansive benevolence that smelled of rye whisky.

Bonal and Seay went straight to the room indicated by Maizie, where the buffet supper was being laid out on two huge tables that abutted one wall. There was a punch, which they both refused for whisky, and drinking it Seay looked over the company. Bonal was already talking to two men.

A string orchestra struck up in an adjoining room. Under the sparkle of the chandelier, people had formed small conversational groups, the sweeping dresses of the women colourful and gay against the uniform black of the men. Seay noticed that most of the women here were middle-aged, although there were many young men. He saw Sharon and Hugh come in and mingle immediately with a group of people who seemed gathered around three girls whom he could not see.

" Finished?" Bonal asked, and Seay said yes, feeling the whisky warm him. " Then let's meet all these people."

Bonal went from group to group, introducing him. These were the men of power in this camp, and their women. For the most part they were amiable, accepting a friend of Charles Bonal's as their own. The younger people all seemed eager for Patti to come, and they waited with impatience.

When she finally did come there was a murmur of excitement in the rooms as word was whispered that she was here. Afterwards Maizie entered, with Patti beside her, and people moved towards them. Beside Maizie Patti was short, and almost girlishly slight, although she was a mature woman. Her yellow evening dress, low cut to expose the olive smoothness of her shoulders, was theatrically conceived and chosen. Her black hair was brushed cleanly off her forehead, and in it she wore a butterfly pin of pearls flanking a huge and flawless emerald. She wore no other jewellery, not even her wedding ring. But it was Patti's eyes that made her beauty—large, black as jet, with long sweeping eyelashes under full black brows. Her straight nose and girlish mouth were patrician, almost haughty, but her smile was as unaffected as that of a Roman flower-girl.

Seay only glimpsed her, and then she was hidden by the people crowding around her.

"A beautiful woman," Bonal murmured, and turned immediately to resume his discussion of milling costs.

Maizie eventually emerged from the crush arm in arm with a woman whom she guided by stages across to where Seay stood, his broad back to her. He felt a hand on his arm and turned to confront her, his tall shoulders hunched a little to hear better.

"This is Phil Seay, Vannie," Maizie said to the woman beside her. "Vannie Shore." Before him Seay saw a woman of about his own age, with hair as black as and sleeker than his own. Her pale blue dress was simple, severe, and there was a warm and reserved friendliness to her smile as if she had already heard of him and liked him before they met. She gave him her hand. It was a full handshake, like a man's, Seay thought, and he regarded her with quiet interest as he murmured the amenities.

"Vannie Shore," he mused. "I'm in your debt for a couple of hundred feet of track, am I not?"

Vannie laughed huskily. "Which hasn't been paid back."

"The Bonal Tunnel doesn't run on a cash basis," Seay replied. "Maybe you've heard that."

"I believe I've heard it mentioned in mining circles," Vannie admitted, and they both smiled. Seay looked over her shoulder to find Sharon Bonal regarding him with a steady stare. She flushed, catching his stare, nodded slightly, and turned away.

Vannie put her arm through Seay's and said, "Shan't we wait until the crowd's let up before you meet the guest?" and Seay agreed.

They found chairs, and Seay sat beside her, and considered her with veiled curiosity. She was watching the room and its movement, at once serene and interested. It came to Seay that this was a strong woman, who had known men and been loved by them, but he searched back through his mind for any remembered mention of her and found only Tober's. She felt his gaze and turned to him and smiled, acknowledging it.

"Have you ever wanted to watch something like this without being watched yourself?" she asked presently.

"I haven't seen enough of them to want to," Seay replied.

"You don't mingle with these people, then?"

Seay shook his head, and Vannie confided, "Neither do I. I only came to-night because of Patti and because Maizie insisted."

"Because of Patti?"

"Yes, she's staying with me to-night. I knew her in San Francisco."

She caught the look of puzzlement in Seay's eyes and she shook her head. "Please don't ask questions. Someone will tell you about me," she said quietly, and there was a note of defiance in her tone.

Seay only frowned and was silent. Presently Vannie leaned towards him and said, "I'm sorry. I didn't mean to be brusque." She regarded Seay now with the same sort of curiosity with which only a moment ago he himself had shown.

"I begin to suspect something," she said at last.

"So do I."

"That Maizie introduced us because we're two of a kind?"

"Perhaps."

"We are, aren't we?" Vannie asked slowly. "You don't like this, nor do I. Moreover, we don't belong here. Isn't that it?"

"You do," Seay answered with quick and inexplicable loyalty. "I don't."

"I don't either, really. Will you have supper with me to-night?"

For answer Seay drawled, "I have a pipe hidden in my pocket, and I'd like a smoke. Do you suppose——?" His voice trailed off as he watched her.

"Yes, I do. Come on."

The couples were just beginning to crowd into the room above, where the buffet supper was laid out. Seay knew they would not be missed. At the foyer door Ben was standing, hands in hip pockets, looking out at the carriages, whistling thinly, and teetering.

"Hallo, Ben," Vannie said, and Ben jerked around and then relaxed. "Hallo, Vannie."

" Do you think you could manage to find your way out here with some food, Ben?" Vannie asked.

" Yes, ma'am," Ben said emphatically. " I already took some out to Hugh Mathias."

" Was that to the right or left?" Vannie asked gravely.

" To the left."

Vannie turned to the right, and they walked down the long stone-flagged porch. Presently she paused and seated herself on the wide balustrade, and Seay stood beside her. His pipe packed and lighted, he inhaled deeply, a strange uneasiness within him. The murmur of the coachmen in some profane argument down by the carriage-house drifted over to them and died, and it was quiet. Two forlorn frogs in the fountain sawed away fitfully.

" How still the night is," Vannie murmured.

" It's a desert night."

" You like it?"

" It's what I've seen most of my life. But I can't imagine liking another kind of night." He was high and remote beside her, his restless face now hard and young in the soft light.

Ben padded out with food on a tray and pulled up a small table.

" Do you want this?" Seay asked abruptly of Vannie.

" No. Why did I ask for it? Convention, I suppose."

" Trot off with it, Ben," Seay said. " Maybe the boys out there would like it."

" That makes two," Ben said delightedly, and went off with the tray, to hurry down the steps and disappear in the direction of the carriages, while Seay and Vannie laughed together. Seay sat on the balustrade now, his curiosity stirring, and watched this woman near him.

Presently Vannie murmured, " Tell me, has Charles Bonal a chance, a desperate chance, to put the tunnel through?"

Seay said, " Yes," promptly, curtly.

" I'm glad," Vannie said, " and not because my good hunch will pay me."

" Pay you?"

" Yes. Jake believed in Bonal before he died, and he loaned him money. I've loaned him more."

Seay didn't comment, but again he found himself trying to recall a name which he knew very well he had never heard.

" You *do* mind your business, don't you?" Vannie murmured, and then she laughed shortly, almost nervously. " You see, I'm trying to tell you about me."

"Then who is Jake?" Seay countered.

Vannie didn't answer immediately. "Jake Fell. He made his fortune and lost it in the rush of '49."

"I've heard of him. Everybody has."

"You see, I lived with him," Vannie said simply. "That's what I'm trying to tell you. His wife was hopelessly insane for thirty years in an asylum back east. We—we just wanted to live together and we did—without marriage. He lived to see the beginning of this Tronah rush, lived long enough to make another fortune in the Golgotha mine and leave it to me."

Seay swiftly came to his feet and stood beside her. "You don't have to do this," he said brusquely. "I know now." Vannie looked away. Sitting down then, facing her, he added, "Yes, we're two of a kind. And bless Maizie Comber for seeing it."

Vannie's laugh was explosively warm and rich as she leaned back against the pillar. "My, but that's a relief. You see, I feel I always have to give fair warning before I can let myself like anybody. It's—it's a kind of protection, I suppose."

Seay was about to answer when Ben appeared out of the darkness.

"They want you in there, Vannie," Ben drawled.

"Why, Ben?"

"This opry singer is aimin' to sing," Ben said. "They figured to have you play the piano."

"Oh," Vannie said shortly, then, "all right, Ben. I'll be in immediately."

When Ben had gone, Vannie sat still a moment, then rose. Seay was beside her. "Look here, Vannie. Where can I see you again?"

"Ask anywhere in town. I live on the primmest street in the primmest house and always keep my shades up." She laughed again, that rich, disturbing laugh that had life and meaning to it and was strangely without bitterness. They walked in silence to the door. Hugh and Sharon were going in, and Sharon saw them. She nodded and said, "Hallo, Vannie," and Hugh spoke in complete friendliness, In those three seconds that Seay watched Sharon, he could see nothing except genuine openness in her manner.

"Tell me," he murmured to Vannie as they stepped inside, "does——?"

Vannie looked swiftly up at him. "Yes, Phil, Sharon really likes me."

Before he could mask the surprise in his face, Vannie let go his arm and moved through the room. Seay stopped at the door, and was glad that he could hang back here, where he would not have to sit before these people, who were crowding into chairs. Vannie walked straight to the ivory and gold piano, and conversed briefly with Patti as the general talking quieted a little. He watched Vannie, not Patti, and he felt a curious pride in this woman.

Sharon Bonal said at his elbow, "Did you hear her to-night?"

Seay turned to find her standing beside him, the fragrance of her close and desirable. A slow hostility began to take hold of him, but her way now was amiable and casual enough, holding neither defiance nor amusement, only a kind of intimate reserve. Without her anger and resentment, which, save for that first night at Union House, had been plain in her face and plainer in her manner. Whenever she saw him, she had a fresh chaste loveliness that almost startled him. He was thinking that it might have been her speech, for the first time kind and welcoming, that made the change.

"I worked too late," he answered.

"I've never heard her before," Sharon went on. "I didn't know singing could be so lovely."

"She's young, isn't she?"

"I don't know. She's almost as beautiful as Vannie, though," Sharon said simply.

Obliquely Seay looked at her, wondering what lay behind this comparison, but Sharon was observing Patti intently.

The first notes of the "*Ah! non giunge*" from *Somnambula* came thin and precise, bringing silence. Seay felt a hand on his arm. Ben stood behind him, face urgent, and he jerked his head toward the foyer.

Sharon saw him, and looked from Ben to Seay as Seay turned and muttered an excuse.

Sharon nodded slightly and he followed Ben out on to the porch. Ben walked rapidly down the steps and turned to the left and Seay caught up with him. "What is it, Ben?"

"I don't know. But it's important, I reckon."

They headed out toward the carriage barns. Under the huge old cottonwood Ben stopped, and Seay brushed into him before he could check his pace. Something moved in the blackness near the trunk and he wheeled to face it.

"Phil?" someone asked, and immediately Seay recognised Jimmy Hamp's voice. His horse shied a little at the noise, and Jimmy pulled him closer.

"Oh," Seay said, his voice chill with dislike.
"You get over to the tunnel," Jimmy said quietly. "Get over fast."
"Why?"
"Trouble."
Seay stepped closer. "What kind of trouble, Jimmy?"
"That's all I can tell you. Get over there and get over fast."
There was quiet menace in Seay's voice as he reached for the reins of Jimmy's horse. "You sold me, Jimmy. Is this another one?"
"*Get over to the tunnel, you bull-headed fool!*" Jimmy said desperately. "It'll be too late to-morrow to believe me when you'll likely find me with a slug in my back."
He wheeled his horse and Seay heard him gallop off toward the barns. For an irresolute second Seay stood motionless, and then he said to Ben, "Saddle me a horse, Ben. And hurry it!"

Chapter VIII

Over toward the tunnel mouth in the light of the flares, men were frantically rigging a hitch for six mules. The string of cars waiting for the mules was already jammed with excited men when Seay rode up and dismounted. He caught sight of Lueter bent over a clevis and he ran toward him. Putting a hand on his shoulder Seay spun him around.
"What's happened?" he asked, his breath coming hard.
"Cave in!" Leuter cried. "Tober's already in there!"
"Are the men trapped?"
"I dunno. I think so. None of 'em came out!"
Seay glanced desperately at his lathered horse. He could ride in, but once the horse was inside, he would only be a hindrance in that crowded tunnel. Clouds of dust started to unfold out of the tunnel mouth and Seay whirled to Leuter.
"What's Tober done?"
"Called out the whole camp."
Seay raised his voice: "Kelly! Kelly!"
Out of the tangle of grim-faced workmen, many trying to light lanterns and still keep a seat on the small cars, Kelly appeared, his face sweating.
"Take half these men and rig up a dump grade just outside the tunnel mouth here," Seay said harshly. "Get a track switch

made as fast as you can. Send a team over to the Consolidated for their smallest hand pump. Get that timbering crew at work turning out timbers as fast as they can, and tell the——"

The train of cars started out with a jerk. Kelly bawled to the men on the last five cars to get down, and as the train of cars disappeared into the tunnel Seay ran alongside and caught on. Two cars up ahead Leuter was standing, and Seay picked his way through these silent men to him. The driver flogged the mules into a trot, and the cars were lurching and clanking deeper into the hot, fetid tunnel.

"Now what happened?" Seay demanded of him above the noise.

"Explosion," Leuter said abruptly. "It was so loud I knew it couldn't be one of the shots in the tunnel head. After that I could hear the stuff slipping. When I got out of the bunk-house, Tober was ahead of me."

"What kind of an explosion?" Seay asked quickly.

"Dynamite."

There was a little dust hanging in the tunnel now. Seay's face held a vast impatience. Much later, in the light from one of the overhead lanterns, Seay saw Tober's long shape gesticulating wildly, and he jumped off the car and ran ahead of the mules. Tober was yelling something, but when Seay passed him he stood for one second in utter amazement and then turned and raced after Seay into the tunnel.

When he had caught up, Seay was standing at the face of the slide. There, from ceiling to roof, the tunnel was blocked by rock and dirt and rubble. A thin fog of dust hung in the still tunnel air, not moving.

Seay stared at this buttress of rock and earth before him. A kind of mental paralysis took hold of him as he thought of Borg Hulteen and his drillers and muckers beyond that wall. How deep was it? He shook himself slightly and looked up. The water pipe had been wrenched from its cleats in the roof, and was so bent under the weight of the dirt that it had buckled.

Now the workmen filed up and viewed the slide in silence. Here, before them, was the miner's chiefest fear—a cave-in. Before it, they stood awed, for here was the old terror, impersonal, savage and final.

Now Seay pulled off his coat, talking to Tober. "That water pipe's no good. But the compressor pipe under the track won't be broken."

"It can't be," Tober said swiftly, and it was almost a prayer.

"Send a car down for tools!" Seay rapped out. "I want that compressor pipe cut about a hundred feet down the tunnel here. I want——"

"It'll fill with water," Tober said quickly. "Borg will think of the compressor pipe. He'll uncouple it from the receiving tank and it'll fill with water!"

"Of course it will!" Seay said savagely. "It's got to fill with water. If it doesn't drain, they'll drown!"

"But the air!" Tober countered.

"They've got enough for a couple of hours, but what good will it do them if they drown!" Seay said savagely. "Call five good men!"

Tober circulated among the waiting workmen and returned with five men.

Seay said swiftly to them, "Go down the tunnel about a hundred feet, boys. In the right-hand wall I want you to cut a station. I want it cut big enough to hold a pump, a four-man suction pump. Get all the help you can use. I want the station cut so the pump will be out of the way of the cars clearing out this muck. You understand?"

Without waiting for their nods of assent, he raised his voice to call, "Who's a machinist here, men?"

Three men left their fellows and came to him. "Now get this straight," Seay said grimly. "How big is the compressor pipe to the receiving tank?"

"Three-inch."

"Have you got a three-inch T-joint in the shops?"

"Sure."

Now Seay talked slowly, his voice rasping with impatience, telling them first what he was trying to do, so they might understand the better what was wanted of them. "Those men back of that cave-in will die of two things, lack of air and drowning. I've got to get air to them, and I've got to pump the water out. You see that?" He pointed down the tunnel. "Down where that station will be put in I'm going to put a suction pump. That pump will connect with the compressor pipe with this three-inch T-joint. You understand?"

They nodded.

"All right. But to get the air to them, I've got to put a half-inch pipe inside the compressor line. Do you get that? One pipe inside another."

Again they nodded.

"Now here's your job." He wanted a plug for one vent of the T-joint. In that plug a hole was to be drilled, a length of half-inch pipe caulked into it. That way the T-joint could be fitted to the end of the compressor line and to the pump, while the air line would continue straight down the tunnel to the good air outside. The water would be pumped out of the compressor pipe; the air line would be carried inside it. When they nodded that they understood, Seay raised his voice. "You men lift a car to the other track and hitch up some mules. These men have got to get to the machine shops!"

When that was done, Seay's patience broke. His voice was hard and driving as he organised the rest of the workmen into mucking crews. Out of that bedlam there was soon order. Shovels, block and tackle for the heavy boulders came. The timbers and the timbering crew appeared. Swiftly the work got under way. One crew worked at the slide, shovelling, lifting, loading it into the dump cars, while the other crew trucked down the tunnel with it. Elbow to elbow with the muckers, the timberers worked, timbering the roof and the walls as the men dug. The air was stifling here, but the men worked in a fury of speed.

Later the suction pump came and work was stopped for five minutes while the pump was stalled into the station where it would be out of the way of the dump cars.

Then the machinists appeared, and they cut the compressor line. Immediately the water gushed out, and Seay felt a vast relief. This meant that Borg had sensed what they would try to do, and had uncoupled the pipe from the receiving tank. And now the whole crew watched while the machinists fed the half-inch pipe through the big compressor pipe. There was not a man here who did not understand that, if this failed, those trapped men would die.

Foot after foot of the slim pipe was fed into the fatter one.

"How much?" Seay demanded of the machinist.

"A third enough."

He waited, his breath coming slow and even as he tried to fight the intolerable strain that was riding him and these men. The pipe went on and on, slowly, slowly.

Suddenly, after long minutes, the pipe suddenly jerked in the machinist's hands. It was the signal that Borg had the other end of it.

The workmen accepted it in different ways. Some of them swore, some of them cheered faintly, and on the face of the rest was a vast and indescribable relief.

The rest was swift. The T-joint was fitted, and joined to the pump. Now the four men swinging the double handles of the pump had a steady stream of water gushing out the pump vent. It was a pathetically small stream to fight the steady seeping of water in at the tunnel head. Now it was a fight with time, and with water, with no way of telling who was winning until it would be too late to help.

Tober, looking at the stream, said, "Is it enough?"

Seay only shook his head. "If we're lucky and reach them in time."

Work now reached a fever pitch. Men laboured in that fogged lantern light until they had to be hauled off, exhausted, by the men on the next shift. His white shirt torn and smeared now, Seay watched the slide recede. The hot stinking air here was almost strangling, and the billows of dust that rolled round the workmen made it worse. Nothing that was uncovered escaped his notice, nor did his gaze once stray from the face of that implacable wall.

When a workman uncovered a shattered timber, Seay was beside him. Next to the timber was the twisted scrap of what had been a dump car. But it was the timber he examined. It had been chewed into slivers by the explosion.

Slowly, Seay turned the timber over, his face reflective, and then told one of the mucking crew, "Haul all the timbers and scrap out and put it under lock and key."

Tober, whose expression was alert, angry, glanced at him. "Dynamite did that," he said quietly.

Seay nodded.

"Kelly found Ahearn, the mule driver, up on the mountain. He'd been slugged in the head," Tober went on.

"What happened to him?"

"He doesn't know. He had a string of empties ready out by the dump and he was putting in a link pin when something landed on his head."

"Ah," Seay said gently, watching Tober. "Could it happen that way?"

"He hitched his empties at the bottom of the dump, three or four hundred yards from the men on the dump."

"In the dark?"

"With only the mule's lantern. A lantern is too unhandy to carry."

Seay said almost gently. "So they slugged him, threw the dynamite in the cars, drove the mules in, planted the stuff, and walked out." He turned away, but Tober grabbed his arm and yanked him round. For a moment they faced each other, not speaking, and then Tober said desperately:

"My God, Phil, can't you see it?"

"Can't I see what?" Seay asked levelly.

"Why, that somebody sold us out again! When you use dynamite in rock like this, you've got to have time! Time to drill your holes! There's only one place they could have put dynamite without drilling so Hulteen wouldn't hear them, and that's where they did!"

"In this timbering we put up the other day?"

"Hell yes!" Tober cried. He paused, and unblinkingly he watched every slight change of expression on Seay's face.

"Yes," Seay said quietly.

"Then how did they know there was a spot they wouldn't have to drill in unless somebody told them—unless one of us sold out!"

Seay didn't answer.

"They didn't come this close to the tunnel head looking for a place to drill!" Tober said vehemently. "Hulteen would have heard them. Don't you see, they *knew* about this shoring, *knew* they wouldn't have to drill! Who told them?"

Seay shrugged wearily.

"Somebody—and this time it could be anyone in camp," Tober said. He turned away, his voice choked with a wild cursing, and walked down the tunnel, and Seay watched him go, understanding him.

Bonal came in once that morning and the next midnight, and he ordered Seay out of the tunnel to sleep and Seay didn't even bother to laugh at him. The crew were working with a wordless fury, and they protested violently when Seay shortened the shifts to ease their weariness. It seemed to him that he had always been here, or that time had stood still for days now. Or was it days? He didn't know and couldn't remember when it was he walked into this dust-fogged tunnel with the knowledge that nine men, walled away from him by part of a mountain, were dependent on him for their lives.

He gnawed at bread and threw it away and drank gallons of coffee laced with whisky. Men left their shifts and slept and came back and he was still cursing the timberers for being in the way of the mucking crew and cursing the mucking crew for delaying the timbering.

He paced the growing space between the pump and the slide until men damned him for a wild man, and still, to him, the work did not go fast enough. Seared in his brain was that picture of nine men in the tunnel, their lamps long since extinguished to save air, feeling, only feeling, the water rise.

Maybe they were lying on the slope of rock, huddled around the bent-up slim pipe where the air was less hot. The heat would be hell there, and they would all be wondering how it felt to drown in hot water. Hulteen would keep them sane with that brutal humour of his, but time, in which there was no day or night, would sap even that. Hunger would have long since been forgotten, and the precious plugs of tobacco which had been hoarded at first would lie soggy and forgotten in their pockets. Only the dim flame of hope would still burn, and it would die soon now. Or maybe, behind that slope of rock and dirt, there were nine bodies stirring only with a slow current that would bump them up against the roof of a sightless cavern. He still had strength enough to forbid this thought any room in his mind, but when it appeared, it was with the slow horror of a corpse rising to the surface. Then he would stride down to the air pipe, placed far down the tunnel in the cooler air, and when he saw it was not running water he would brace himself again and go back.

By the third day Bonal was only an insistent puppet who appeared at intervals to harass him with words and then leave.

It was when it all became a jumble of Borg, of lanterns and pipes and Bonal and muck and track and clean-smelling timber and dust and pumps that he was staring at the slide face when he heard a man cry out. He didn't understand what the man said, but he looked to where the man was pointing. There, in the tunnel floor, the dirt was beginning to blot up water. The men were standing around staring at it with red-rimmed stupid eyes when Seay shouted, "Get out of the way!"

The dirt blotted water faster until a trickle started and then a stream spurted out and men leapt to the side of the tunnel.

And then the whole geyser burst out of the face and after it a waist-high wall of water, and Seay was swept off his feet and carried down the tunnel. He saw a man ride out on that wall of water, arms flailing, and behind him, another man tumbled out and fell face down and was washed clear and then one of the mucking crew swung a lantern over his head and splashed into the current, which was lessening. A shout was joined by another and Seay staggered to his feet and tried to run.

They were alive, the nine of them. Hulteen was on his knees, the water runnelling around him, his face screwed up with pain and his fists rammed in his eyes.

"Take that light away!" he cried hoarsely, and Seay laughed.

Down the tunnel a string of empty dump cars was trundled back and the nine men loaded on them. Some of them were laughing, and others were sobbing, while around them the joyful and cursing workmen slapped each other on the back and cursed again with delight.

Seay swung on a car and rested his hand on Hulteen, who looked up at him and shook his head and grinned and said nothing, his head hung.

Outside, the whole camp was jamming the tunnel mouth, and the men were soon carried away. Seay saw Tober and he walked over to him, weaving on his feet, and said, "Get me a horse, Reed. I want a horse, too. Get me a gun."

Tober opened his mouth and turned his head to yell and then he whipped around to catch Seay, who had fallen into him. He stood him on his feet again, and for three brief seconds Seay's legs tried to take the weight and couldn't. He collapsed.

Tober, grinning, let him slack to the ground, and rose and bawled joyfully, "Give me a lift, you buckos, and shag it!"

Chapter IX

Hugh Mathias's secretary took Charles Bonal's hat and said, "Mr. Mathias would like to see you in the board room, Mr. Bonal."

Bonal strode toward the door marked, H. Mathias, Manager, and the secretary said quickly, "Not through there, Mr. Bonal, please. Follow me."

Scowling, Bonal followed the secretary, who left the anteroom, turned right at the corridor, and down it stopped at the second door and opened it. The room was large, holding only a huge table flanked by a dozen chairs. Three large pictures of the Dry Sierras buildings decorated the wall. Hugh Mathias was standing before one of the windows smoking a cigar, and when the door opened he whirled to see who it was. Dropping his cigar, he came swiftly around the table and shook hands with Bonal.

"I couldn't receive you in the office, Bonal. There's a man in there I didn't want you to see until I could talk to you." His face was drawn, its agitation plain.

"What did you want to see me about, Hugh?"

"I've got to be brief," Hugh said, talking in a low voice. "You know, of course, about that market flurry last week when they were hammering our stock."

"You told me about it." He was quietly curious.

Hugh reached in his pocket and brought out a telegram and handed it to Bonal. "I got this last night, late. It's from our attorney in 'Frisco. It simply says that after the smoke cleared on the market the other day, a Mr. Barton McCauley showed up with enough Dry Sierras stock and voting proxies that I'd better pay attention to him. It also says McCauley has a man on the way to Tronah." Hugh gestured toward the office. "He's in there now. A lawyer—Freehold by name."

Bonal read the telegram and handed it back to Hugh and asked quietly, "How does that concern me?"

"He asked me to send for you."

"What for?"

"All he would say was that it was a business matter of some importance that concerned us both."

Bonal said, "All right, let's see him."

Hugh put down his cigar and showed Bonal to the corridor. In the ante-room once more he held the door to his office open and Bonal walked inside. A spare, tall man was seated at a chair drawn up next to Hugh's chair. Hugh introduced them, and put a chair for Bonal facing the desk. His office was large, pleasant, simple.

Freehold carefully lighted a cigar, not looking at Bonal, who was studying him with a belligerent curiosity.

"Mr. Bonal," Freehold said in an expressionless voice, "I've made this trip for two purposes—to examine the books of this mining company and to talk with you."

"I'm here," Bonal said, his voice expressing no pleasure in that fact.

"So are the books," Freehold replied, gesturing with a burned match to the open ledger on the desk. "These books tell me that the Dry Sierras holds your notes due to be called next week sometime. Is that correct?"

Bonal nodded. "As far as it goes. However, I was assured that any time I wanted a ninety-day extension on it, I could get it, supposing a one per cent increase in the rate of the interest was agreeable to me. It is."

"Have you that in writing, Mr. Bonal?" Freehold inquired.

Hugh put in quickly, "No. It was simply a gentleman's agreement."

Freehold regarded Hugh with a polite tolerance. "Between whom, may I ask?"

"Bonal and myself."

"And you acted in what capacity?"

"As chairman of the board," Hugh said, his irritation mounting. " I'm empowered to make loans with a certain per cent of the surplus, and I act with the consent of two-thirds of the directors."

" Would it interest you to know?" Freehold asked, " that at the meeting of the stockholders next month, the personnel of the board will be changed."

" You mean I'm to be removed?" Hugh asked quickly.

" That depends."

Hugh came forward in his chair and said, " On what does it depend, Mr. Freehold?"

Freehold said idly, " The group I represent, Mr. Mathias, headed by Barton McCauley, has the voting power to remove you as chairman of the board. If we do so, it will be because you refuse to act in accordance with our wishes. We represent the majority of stockholders, of course."

" And what are your wishes?" Hugh demanded.

Freehold's gaze touched Bonal and then settled again on Hugh. " That the notes of Bonal, held by us, shall be called on the specified dates and not renewed."

Bonal grunted. His beard hid any expression in his face, and he sat utterly motionless.

Hugh's face flushed. " Let me call to your attention, Freehold," he said quickly, " that I'm chairman until the board meeting following the stockholders' meeting. That will be some weeks off." He leaned back in his chair. " Those notes come due before that, and I will certainly renew them."

" I was afraid of that," Freehold said. " You will be served with an injunction restraining you."

" On what grounds?"

" That it's unwarranted gambling with company funds. I already have a stockholders' petition before the judge. He can't very well deny the injunction."

Hugh said hotly, " And my attorney will start suit to make you show cause why——"

Bonal said abruptly, " No, son, no!"

Hugh turned to him and Bonal raised a hand. " Let me talk, please." He turned to Freehold and asked, " What objection is there to renewing my notes?"

Freehold smiled thinly. " You asked for it, Mr. Bonal. It's this. We feel that it would be less risk to back a roulette game without money than to lend it to the Bonal Tunnel scheme."

" Why?"

Freehold shrugged. " Intrinsically, it's unworkable, we think."

"You mean, Janeece thinks so."

Freehold said evenly, "I don't recall that his name is listed among the stockholders I represent. We simply refuse to gamble."

Bonal nodded gently. "All right. There's no use of your resorting to the courts. I understand that my notes will be called at maturity, with no chance of renewal."

"But there is!" Hugh said hotly. "They can't——"

"They can," Bonal cut in. He spoke to Hugh now, his voice suddenly gentle. "I appreciate your loyalty, Hugh, but there's no reason to jeopardize your career in a fight you're sure to lose." To Freehold, he said, "Let's have your report read that Mathias disagreed with you, but that he'll be willing to abide by the decision of the new directors. Shall we?"

Freehold nodded. "I think so." He rose, shook hands with both men, instructed Hugh that he would receive written orders before two days were up, and let himself out.

When he was gone, Hugh looked soberly at Bonal, who was sitting back in his chair, his eyes veiled and brooding.

Hugh said bitterly, "And that's how I keep my word."

Bonal stirred, and sighed. "That's how most of us do, Hugh. We try, and that's all."

"It's rotten," Hugh said quietly.

"It's business." He rose and took out a cigar and lighted it and his beard was out-thrust, as if he were ashamed to have Hugh witness this moment of defeat. "Well, to hell with it," he said mildly, as he threw his match on the rug. "I can meet the notes and have some funds left over."

"But not enough to complete the tunnel?"

Bonal shook his head, and they were both silent. Presently Bonal said, "Don't take it so hard, son. I've fought these scabby rats all my life. I've got a few tricks to take yet."

"But the tunnel."

Bonal looked up and his eyes were grim. "They're still working on it, aren't they?"

He got his hat in the outer office and went out to the buggy. From here he could look down on the town laid out untidily below him. The morning sun was not kind to it, and it lay ragged in all its hot ugliness. Bonal paid no attention to the activity behind him up the slope, where the dump cars were clanging out of the shaft house. The labouring hoist engine filling the still air with its bustling and the sacked ore was being loaded on to the freight teams to one side of the shaft house.

In the buggy going down the winding grade to the town, he chewed reflectively on his cigar. Strangely, he felt a pity for Hugh Mathias, who had yet to learn that business and friendship do not mix. At any rate, Hugh had helped to tide him over the darkest moments, when the tunnel seemed impossible to get under way. He had loaned money until his directors had called a halt. Tools, equipment, men, money—everything that made the tunnel a fact, Hugh Mathias had gladly given, for he had a faith in the tunnel that was next to his own, Bonal believed. Sharon would hate this, mostly for Hugh's sake, and Hugh would tell her in an agony of shame. Better tell her before he got the chance, Bonal thought wearily. Back of thought, he wondered with an old man's surfeit of life if he would ever have rest from trouble. Misfortune dogged the tunnel with an implacability that sometimes frightened him. No, that wasn't entirely true. There were nine men over the mountain here, alive because he had the good fortune—or sense—to hire Phil Seay. The thought of Seay warmed something inside Bonal, and gave him a kind of impersonal strength. There was *his* kind of man, with a hard belly and hard fists and a brain inside his hard skull, a man who would rather fight than eat, and who had the strength to be gentle. Bonal remembered him as they carried him down to the bunk-house after Hulteen and his men were freed. He lay there in the same clothes he left Maizie Comber's party in three nights before, and he was already a thousand miles deep in sleep, and yet he contrived to be as stubborn and unyielding in sleeping as some men are in waking. Charles Bonal laughed quietly, so that his driver looked quickly at him and then away. There was a frank envy in Bonal as he thought of it, and he sighed a little, remembering that all he could share with Seay was the pleasure of the fight, and none of its healthy lust. Damn the years.

At the Union House he mounted the stairs to his suite with his indomitable deliberation, and entered the corner room he called his office. Sharon heard him enter and called to him from another room, and when she came in he was seated at the desk. She kissed him and sat on the desk, and she looked so fresh and lovely that he did not have the heart to tell her of Hugh's misfortune.

"Dad, will you take me to the tunnel this afternoon?" Sharon was saying, and she had to repeat it before Bonal asked why. "But I've heard nothing for five days except about the cave-in. Can't I see it?"

" Half-naked?" Bonal inquired, for Maizie had told him of Seay's retort.

Sharon blushed and then laughed delightedly, and Charles Bonal felt better.

" So Maizie told you?" Sharon said. " That man has got a horrible mind."

" He's got a mind," Bonal admitted. " It's not always——"

There was a hammering on the outside door, and it was imperative. Bonal started to rise when Sharon skipped off the desk and went over and opened the door.

Reed Tober strode in. He went straight to Bonal's desk and leaned both hands on it and said, " Bonal, you've got to stop him!"

" Who?" Bonal asked quickly. " Seay?"

" Yes. He's huntin' every saloon in town now, kickin' doors in and not a man on the streets will touch him."

" Is he drunk?" Sharon asked swiftly.

Tober turned to her, his eyes wide, staring. " Drunk? No, ma'am, I wisht he was. I could hit him then." He turned back to Bonal. " I can't stop him. He'd kill me."

" Who is it he's looking for?" Bonal said.

" I think it's Feldhake. When he woke up this mornin', he dressed and took his gun and rode over here and he's on the prod." Tober shook his head pleadingly. " If you can't do it, don't try, Bonal, but we got to stop him."

" Where is he?" Sharon asked.

" I dunno. One of the saloons. He'll make them all until he finds him, and when he does he'll kill him and that's all Janeece wants. That's all he'll need. He won't care about witnesses or about a reason. He'll kill him."

" Who won't care?" Sharon cried, exasperated at Tober's jumbled speech.

Again Tober turned to her, his face almost surprised. " Why, him, ma'am."

" Where is Yates?" Bonal asked harshly. " Can't he stop him?"

" He don't want to," Tober said emphatically. " He's told him to quit it. Now all he wants is for him to pull that gun—just pull it."

" But I can't do anything, Reed," Bonal said wearily. " For four days he laughed at me whenever I told him to leave the tunnel." He rose and reached for his hat on the corner of the desk.

"We got to stop him," Tober said stubbornly. "We got to——"

"Dad, let me do it!" Sharon said swiftly. "The sight of a woman will stop him! You'd only make him worse! So would Tober!"

Reed looked at her as if he had just this moment noticed her.

"Nonsense," Bonal said sharply. "I won't have you mixing in street brawls."

Sharon turned and ran toward the door and Bonal called her. Tober stood for five irresolute seconds, and then he wheeled and ran after her and Bonal shouted angrily at him.

On the Union House porch Tober caught up with her.

Sharon said breathlessly, "Which way?"

Tober took her arm and almost carried her along, turning up the street as if hurrying to some momentous appointment. People on the crowded sidewalk turned to stare at them. Little knots of knowing men had already come to stop in eddies near the buildings, waiting for what was going to happen. It was one of these men who reached and hooked Tober's arm and stopped him, saying, "He's in Sig Pool's shop, Reed. Two men took him in."

"Two——" Reed began, and then he shook loose the man's restraining arm and ran, leaving Sharon. Sig Pool's was a barber shop. When Tober crashed in, swinging the door open, he had a gun in one hand, and his momentum carried him close to the chair where Sig was shaving a man. Sig pointed with a razor to the door in the back wall, and Tober strode over to it and flung the door open, Sharon behind him.

Two rough-looking men leaned against the far wall. Seay was standing, legs spread, in front of the window. And close to him, talking to him, was Vannie Shore. They all looked over as the door opened, and watched Reed's face settle into a kind of dogged sheepishness before he holstered his gun.

Sharon, who came close on Tober's heels, and Vannie regarded each other a long moment, and Sharon felt the blood creeping up into her face.

"I——" she began, and stopped, and her impulse was to turn and run, but Tober blocked the door—and besides, her pride would not let her. Her gaze touched Seay's face, sardonic, determined, shaped by the raging impatience in his eyes. And then Sharon looked back at Vannie, who was smiling now.

"Maybe you can make him listen, Sharon," Vannie said

quietly. She turned to the two men and said, "Come on, boys. And thank you." The three of them left, and Tober closed the door behind them. Sharon walked slowly over to Seay, who had not moved, whose attitude proclaimed that he could bear this pause too.

"Father wants to see you at the hotel," Sharon said falteringly.

"Afterwards," Seay said.

"No, now." And then suddenly, Sharon lost all the stiffness that had gripped her, and some of the pride too. "Oh, Phil, how can you gamble with so much?" she said passionately. "So much that isn't yours!"

Seay's eyes widened a little but he spoke without heat and with a patience that was unbearable to watch. "Those nine men were mine to keep alive. That tunnel is mine to put through."

"But can't you see, that is what they want?" Sharon cried. "Have you got to fall into their clumsy traps like a bullied schoolboy?"

Seay's face darkened and his lips drew tight across his teeth. Then slowly he exhaled his breath in a great gust.

"They want you to do this, Phil. Yates is out there with a hundred witnesses. He warned you," Sharon said desperately.

Seay shifted his wicked gaze to Tober. "Did he?"

"He talked to you for three minutes," Tober said quietly. "You laughed at him."

"You haven't a chance, Phil," Sharon pled. "Don't you see, it wasn't the tunnel they were after the other night. It was you! They *knew* you would do this. And you are. Are you?"

Seay said nothing, his hot eyes still on Tober.

"You'll never get the chance to meet this man you're hunting. When you see him, Yates will shoot you. He can. And if he does, where will the tunnel be—or Dad, or Reed, or your nine men, or all the men?"

Seay's glance whipped back to her. "Where are they now? With not a man's life safe!"

Sharon shook her head, looking into his eyes. "You can't, Phil! If you kill him, other men like him can be bought! It wouldn't settle anything—it would only destroy it!"

Seay turned and looked out the window, which opened on to the blank side of the adjoining building. The room was touched with the oversweet scent of barber's lotions that clung to the discarded bottles and jars heaped in the corner and mingled with the old hot dust of the place. Sharon turned her head to look at Reed, and Reed nodded imperceptibly.

Seay swung around slowly and said, "All right. I—you're right."

Sharon put a hand on his arm and smiled a little. "It's too simple—too open to walk into." Seay did not look at her, he reached out for his hat that lay on the dusty packing case, and then turned to her, his face contained and normal. "That's right," he said quietly.

Sharon was trembling a little, but she managed to say offhandedly, "Dad really does want to see you. Will you go with me?"

Seay nodded. Sharon walked out between them. Once on the sidewalk, Reed was on one side of her and Seay on the other. The knowing men lining the streets turned or looked away, and Sharon flushed deeply at what she knew they were thinking. Seay tramped beside her, face grave, speaking to no one.

In front of the Union House, the sidewalk was cleared, and while Sharon was still wondering why, she stepped into the cleared space and then looked at Tober. He was slowing his pace, his glance directed to the hotel porch.

Towering against the pillar, his attitude at once casual and wary, was Chris Feldhake. Sharon had never seen him before, but she immediately sensed that it was he. She felt Tober's fingers clasp her wrist and pull, but she fought it quietly and with all her strength. Tober came to a stop then and Seay did too, and Sharon stayed beside him.

"You lookin' for me, Seay?" Feldhake drawled, his voice insolent, contemptuous, above the street noise.

Sharon waited for what Seay was going to say. She did not look at him, for she did not want to humiliate him before these men, before Feldhake.

She was surprised at the easy readiness of his answer.

"Not yet, Chris."

Feldhake straightened up. "I heard you wanted to see me," he drawled. "I thought they must be wrong." Slowly he raised his hand to put the cigar in his mouth.

"I said, not yet," Seay said again, the slightest edge on his voice.

Feldhake grinned, raised a finger to his hat in the first sign of recognition he had given Sharon, and then swung down off the steps and headed downstreet.

Sharon felt a hand guiding her elbow and she mounted the steps. It was not until they were in the half light of the stairwell that she dared look at Seay. His face was pale and the muscles along his jaw-line corded with an effort that she understood, but his expression was reserved, remote.

"Thank you," she murmured.

"I learn my lessons well—once I learn 'em," he answered lightly.

Sharon left him at Charles Bonal's door and went down to her room and closed the door behind her.

Sinking down on her bed, she stared at the rug and did not try to fight the steady feeling of shame that crept through her, making her angry and disgusted. It was only minutes since that she came out of a barber shop on the arm of a man who an hour ago she thought she despised. Now she knew that she had never despised him, and that events had betrayed her and finally trapped her into this final humiliation. She rose and moved restlessly to the window and looked out, and then she remembered that she had seen him do this a little while ago. She came away then and sat on the bed again, waiting for this turmoil to settle in her mind. She wanted to call herself cheap, for she held that what she had just done was unwomanly. Hugh would think so too, although he would defend her. And then she thought of Vannie Shore, who had done the same thing, and probably with no thought of opinion, and she recalled that pang of bitter jealousy felt as she came up beside Reed Tober in that back room and found Vannie and Seay there. Wanting to honestly understand herself, she went back over every word she had said. She had called him Phil; a day ago she would not have spoken his name. Why? What had changed her save the excitement of that minute when Tober stammered out his helplessness to her father? It was more than that. She had pled with a conviction that appalled her now because she knew it had been sincere.

The answer was slow in dawning on her, because she fought it at every turn, and with all those weapons of scorn and pride that she could command. Later, when she rose and walked over and seated herself in front of the mirror and looked at her reflection, it was to study her face intently, without vanity. It was not the face of a common woman, or an indecisive woman. For one fleeting instant, she thought she recognised a new and strange tranquillity there, and her memory leaped to Vannie Shore. Yes, Vannie's face was tranquil, serene.

But when she groped for the reason for it, she remembered

Vannie and Phil Seay at Maizie's party. Could Vannie's serenity have its source in that night? And what that thought led to made Sharon stand up so abruptly that she knocked over the stool she had been sitting on. She went out swiftly, her face dark with shame.

Chapter X

Borg Hulteen was roaming the way between the two bunk-houses, his eyes on the bunk-house doors, a slab of bread and ham in his fist. It was a half hour yet till the shift change at the tunnel-head, but Borg was hunting up his crew, ordering them one by one away from their brief rest into the tunnel. By six, before six, he would have them at work.

Seay stepped to the door of the office and called to him, and Borg tramped over, chewing morosely on the tag end of his supper. Seay was already seated in the doorway, and Borg sat down beside him. From one side of his mouth, he emptied a considerable accumulation of tobacco juice; that done, he chewed again on the bread and ham.

"Hot, hunh?" he commented.

"I talked with Bonal this noon," Seay said. "They've got him on the run again."

"Money?"

"Yes."

"How far can we get with what we've got?"

"That depends on you," Seay said. "We've got enough for a month's expenses, Bonal says."

Borg was quiet a moment. "We can turn it into two if you'll keep them process servers away from the tunnel-head." Borg grinned suddenly. "Hell, come to that, we could store enough grub in there to make it three—if you could still keep them out of the tunnel."

Seay smiled meagrely. "It may come to that. I fought with Bonal to lay part of that money on equipment. If we got the drills, we can fight court orders for a long time. Providing, of course"—and here he looked swiftly at Borg—"that the men will take a wage cut and maybe no wages at all toward the last."

"I know nine men that will," Borg answered slowly.

"It may come to that and I hate to do it."

Borg rose and wiped his mouth with a hairy forearm.

"Maybe I'm wrong, Phil, but I think we're workin' into a new formation there at the head—softer rock."

Seay looked up at him. "You sure?"

Borg nodded. "I ain't one of these experts with a hammer, but I can tell how it drills. This is softer. Besides, the colour's different. I'll know better to-night when I come off."

When Borg was gone, Seay sat on the sill, turning over in his mind the implications of what Borg had just told him. But he refused to count on luck and he rose and returned to the office. On the desk was the time-sheet, his legacy from Hardiston. When he thought of that spare, vicious little man, the old anger boiled up in him, but it was an impotent anger now. Not even Tober guessed that it was Hardiston who had sold the tunnel information to Feldhake—sold it twice, this last time out of revenge for being detected in selling it the first time. Nor did Bonal, who accepted Seay's word that the desert heat was breaking the little man, and that he had been sent to the coast for a vacation.

Fighting his restlessness, he concentrated on the time-sheet, the pen fragile and strange in his square hand. Whenever he was forced to do this, it was a compromise with his temper, for he had no liking for this work. He went at it much like a schoolboy, concentrating fiercely, shoulders hunched, with an attention that was too absorbing to be of any long duration. At dark he lighted the lamp and worked on, but slowly his interest lagged and he found himself unable to give the work even his easiest attention. Thoughts kept intruding with such insistence that finally he threw his pen down, swore at the smear he had made on the time-sheet, and rose. Craig could finish it. This was his kind of work, or work that he had resigned himself to doing.

At the door of the office he looked out over the camp. By lantern light, a few men were pitching horseshoes down by the warehouse. The lights in the cook-shack still burned, but the clatter had died. The bunk-houses were already quiet, crude slab temples dedicated alike to sleep. Up at the tunnel mouth he could see the new guards conversing. Somewhere out in the night Reed Tober was prowling ceaselessly, alert for any trouble.

Seay turned back to the office, and all at once its hot loneliness was unbearable. Blowing out the light, he took his hat and went out, and found himself turning towards the stables. He smiled at this, wondering if this was what had been in the back of his mind these last two hours.

He was saddling his horse in the dark when Tober came up silently and said, "Phil!"

Seay grunted. Both Tober and Bonal had pled with him to avoid Tronah, to stay away from its crowds. They had good reason, he had admitted to them then, but to-night he was in a mood to ignore it. Waiting for Tober to speak up again, he finished saddling and led his horse out of the pole corral.

"You got a gun?" was all Tober said.

Seay told him no, and he accepted the one Tober gave him and rammed it in his belt. He stepped into the saddle then, and Tober stood away while he rode down the rough street and angled up the road towards the pass.

It came to him that it was excitement he wanted to-night, a change. Gambling maybe. And when he thought of gambling, he thought immediately of what Sharon Bonal had said of his gambling. Resentment stirred within him and then vanished, and he let memory frame the image of her there in the back room of Sig Pool's barber shop. She had been without pride then, and he probed his memory for what she had told him, but it was not clear. But he still remembered her face, alive for once with a grave concern that went beyond consideration of him and his stubborn rage. It had been a sudden loyalty to her father that had broken that pride. He remembered, too, the quiet way she faced Feldhake, the iron of her presence turning Feldhake's threat into cheap bluster, an unpleasant incident encountered on the streets. And her own contagious conviction then had given him the power to laugh, and looking back on it now he smarted under the memory of his own foolhardiness of the minutes before. When she had thanked him for that, it was without reproof that his own violence had threatened her with a street brawl and worse. It occurred to him then that her pride was not broken at all, and that the spirit of her was not brittle or false, but like a flame that burned high in still air, that bent and weaved but did not die against the pressure it sometimes met. This was a woman of Charles Bonal's kind, indomitable and proud and unconquered, and not easy. Not easy. Memory of the times he had seen her before, when his own impulse and deed was to jeering anger and her own was to an overriding his, made him smile thoughtfully into the night. His rough ways irritated her, and he in turn was impatient of her dominating him as if he were one of those soft and agreeable men who seemed to surround her. Still, Hugh Mathias was not wholly soft, although there was behind his affability a seeming unease that puzzled Seay. Wealth and breeding did not hide it. Perhaps its source had been the secret knowledge that sooner or later he was to be the instrument of another one of Charles Bonal's defeats.

Seay pondered this as he packed and lighted his pipe, and lifted one foot out of the stirrup to stretch. The stars were close to-night, and the heat giving off from the rocks around him seemed to lift towards the night sky in invisible waves that made these stars dance fitfully. A rat scurried off in the stunted brush by the road and his horse shied, and he spoke sharply to him.

How would Sharon Bonal face this bad news from Hugh? Like a woman whose love has already acknowledged the imperfections of her man, and to whom forgiving is now easy because at first it was so hard? Abruptly he was angry with himself, and put Sharon Bonal and Hugh Mathias out of his mind.

Approaching Tronah, as he was passing the humble street of miners' homes, he heard the provocative, throaty laugh of a woman hidden in the shadows of a tiny porch, and it disturbed him oddly. For a brief moment fancy tried to explain the reason for that laugh, husky, teasing, warm, and immediately he thought of Vannie Shore. That might have been her laugh.

He reined in a little, his face musing, and he rammed his cold pipe in his pocket. Of a man on a side street, away from the town's clamour, he found where Vannie lived. Anyway, he thought, here is a woman who will let me thank her in my way for a friendly service.

The street was ugly, the afterthought of the town's greed, and it ran aimlessly beyond the alley which separated it from the town's main street. Its houses, some of cut stone, were close to the street, and iron and picket fences tried to cover up the meagreness of the bare yard.

It was at one of these that Seay dismounted and looped the reins of his horse over the iron hitch-rail in front.

The house was dark, but he could make out a white blur on the porch which moved and then became immobile as he opened the gate.

"I wondered if you asked questions for nothing," Vannie Shore greeted him at the steps. "Would you rather sit out here? It's hot inside."

Seay murmured something and took the half of the leather-cushioned porch sofa that was vacant beside Vannie, letting her first pick up the knitting she had laid there.

She did not speak for a moment, but her silence did not

come from awkwardness; it was that she found it hard to shake the habits of loneliness, Seay thought, and thinking it, he asked gently, "You have no one with you, Vannie?"

"Cats," Vannie said. "Cats and knitting." She laughed easily, warmly. "I'm almost into the ways of a widow woman, Phil."

"Rot," Seay said quickly.

Vannie put her knitting aside and stretched out her long, full legs now, and rested her head on the back of the sofa. Seay watched her, unable to see her fully, but the rich fragrance of her was all around him in the night, and he felt his blood strangely quickened.

"Not so much rot as you think," Vannie said quietly. "Maybe I like it." She was silent a moment, and then added more softly, "Maybe I have to like it, so it's just as well."

"But you like men," Seay mused. "They like you. They can't help it."

"It's the women," Vannie said, and without bitterness. "All the men I would like have women—here or somewhere else. And the women here have made it hard for them to know me." She looked lazily towards him. "All except you."

"And I can't—not as often as I'll want to."

"That's the trouble," Vannie said with gentle irony. "The men I would like haven't time for me. And that's all right too. I'd only expect them to have time for me if they more than liked me."

"You make it hard for me to thank you for this morning, Vannie," Seay replied, and his tone held a good-natured truculence. "This is a rough town, where a man hasn't time to take a step for fear he'll take his foot off the neck of the man below him." He said more seriously, "Why don't you leave, then?"

"I own a mine."

"A man could run it for you."

"Not so well. Besides, it's the one thing I hold to—a kind of lifeline keeps me from drowning in self-pity. For ten hours a day I'm alive with a sense of power, success. I'm thankful for that. What happens during the rest of the day isn't so bad," she added, looking full at him. "You must know the feeling, Phil. It's almost your life."

"Not the self-pity."

"Nor mine. I say it keeps me from it. And you're not a woman, so you wouldn't know about that part of it."

Seay rose and walked over to the single step and rammed his hands in his hip pockets, his old restlessness upon him. The things Vannie said always had the power to disturb him. He said over his shoulder, "Tell me, Vannie. Is self-pity the lot of a woman?"

"Of my kind, unless we're careful," she said after some consideration.

"Your kind?"

"Yes, the kind that gives like a man, wants like a man, and yet has to play out her life being a woman."

He half-turned to her, roused by something close to passion in her voice, and Vannie knew it and said more. "There are women, Phil, who can be ladies all their lives until once their pride cracks because of a man, and they let him have that human glimpse of them. And there are some men who are so used to that ladylikeness that they are confounded by the glimpse of humanity. That is what they call love."

A faint anger stirred within him, and curiosity too, for he read this to mean Sharon Bonal and her actions this morning. If he had thought this same thing, drawing no conclusions from it, then Vannie had supplied those conclusions for him.

"Pin that down, Vannie," he murmured, walking towards her.

"Do I have to??"

"Yes."

"I meant Sharon."

He looked down at her, strangely without anger. "How?" he asked. "How?"

Vannie rose now to face him. "Phil, is your memory so short that——?" She paused. "How short is it? *So* short is it?"

Seay didn't answer.

"Do you want me to tell you what she said to you this morning, Phil? She said that you were acting like a boy, that you were playing out a hand that Servel Janeece had dealt you, and the way he wanted you to. She said that you were carrying more than your own life on your shoulders. She said to wait, wait for the time when you were free to square your accounts. Didn't she? Didn't she say that?"

Seay said angrily, "You were listening?"

Vannie laughed shortly. "Not listening, Phil. I know, because I said the same thing to you myself not a minute before she came. And which of us did you listen to?" She paused and he could hear her laboured breathing. "You listened to her, Phil. You didn't even hear me. And you didn't hear me because you knew that was what I would say. Tober had said it already. You'd already said it to yourself, but you were so stubborn you couldn't hear. It took Sharon Bonal to make you listen."

"You hate her, Vannie?" Seay murmured.

"Not hate her. I envy her," Vannie said bitterly. "She gives so seldom that, when she does, it can startle you to life. I give because it's my way, Phil—a man's way, Tober's way, your way—but you can't hear me. Don't you call that love?"

Seay gripped her arms tightly. "Don't say that!"

"I'll say that and more," Vannie said quietly. "Wake up, Phil. You're a grown man, and know yourself. I've known it since I first set eyes on you at Maizie's. You were friendly with me because I was friendly with you and you were starved for kindness from a woman, a handsome woman. And all the time you were being so grateful to me for liking you, you were thinking of Sharon Bonal and her pride, watching for her, hungering to be tramped on. And when she threw you one bone to-day, you are so grateful—so pathetically grateful."

Seay shook her in his anger.

"That's right," Vannie said, her voice breaking. "God help me if it isn't! And I could give you much more than the pitiful little she gave you, Phil. That's what hurts. I could give you love. I could warm you with it, Phil, so that the sight of her cold little pride would turn you back to me. I could give you so much—if you only wanted it!"

Slowly Seay let go her arms, and then she was close to him, her arms around him, her head against his shoulder. For a moment she held him so, and then she raised her face to his. The warm softness of her lips was like a drug rioting through him, and he could feel the soft fullness of her body next him; and then, bringing his hands up, he roughly freed himself of her arms.

Vannie was conquered. She stepped back and turned away, and Seay put a hand on her arm and drew her around.

"It's no good, Vannie," he said huskily. "I—it's no good."

"I know," Vannie murmured, watching his face a still moment. "I didn't think it would be. I—I had to fight, that's all."

"It wouldn't work."

"Oh, it would, Phil!" she said passionately. "It would——" She ceased talking, and Seay could feel the spirit go out of her. He stepped over and picked up his hat, and came back to her.

Vannie said, "If you apologise for kissing me, Phil Seay, I

will hate you!" She laughed shortly. "Besides, it was I who kissed you."

Seay put a hand on her arm. "Believe me, Vannie. It wouldn't work. If I thought it would——"

"I know. You are full of her, Phil. Well, go on, and God bless you, you poor fool. And when you know her, Phil, and if it isn't too late, I'll be here."

When the tramping of boots in the harness-room approached the door and he could hear the fumbling with the lock, Hardiston groped in the dark for his gun. He found it and sat bolt upright, holding it awkwardly, cringing back against the dusty oat sacks.

The door opened and light washed the room. The lantern moved into the room, and above it, Hardiston could see the thick, high shoulders of Chris Feldhake. Feldhake swung the lantern high to look around him, and he grunted at sight of Hardiston on top of the oat sacks stacked almost ceiling high. Then he set the lantern on the floor in the middle of the cleared space among the sacked feed, and turned and watched while four other men followed him into the room. The last one closed the door.

Hardiston knew three of them, not by name but by sight. They were the three who always came in with Feldhake, who had come in this room a dozen times in the last four days—hard, quiet men who let Feldhake talk and ask questions. The fourth man was always someone new, and the questions Feldhake asked of this fourth man were always the same. Hardiston lay back on the feed sacks, waiting for the questioning to begin. His face was stubbled with a grey-black beard, and his black suit was powdered with dust. He scratched continually at the oat husks that had worked into his clothes, his hair. He listened now.

"Kirk, you was drivin' a carriage that night out at Comber's party, wasn't you?" Feldhake began. Hardiston turned his head to look down at the men below. Feldhake half-sat on a feed sack. The stranger stood by the lantern. The other three lounged against the door and squatted against feed sacks.

"Sure. The Widowses were out there that night."

"You boys were out in the carriage-house eatin' what Ben brought out to you, weren't you?" Feldhake went on in a casual voice.

"Not in it. We was talkin' there by the wall," Kirk said.

"You see anybody ride up on a saddle-horse durin' the

evenin'?" Feldhake asked. Hardiston looked over at him. He had a straw stuck in his mouth, his hat cuffed back off his forehead. His face was sleepy, brutal, almost smiling, but he contrived to give an unobservant man the impression of wholly friendly curiosity.

"Yeah, I seen a man ride up," Kirk said slowly, trying to recall. "Why?"

"Remember who it was?"

"I never paid no attention," Kirk said.

Feldhake shifted his thick shoulders faintly and went on. "He was ridin' a buckskin, wasn't he?"

"Yeah, that's right."

"Hear him say anything?"

Kirk scowled now and took off his hat and scratched his head. He was a middle-aged man with an amiably plain face.

"Yeah, he asked us to send Ben over."

"You wouldn't remember the voice?" Feldhake persisted gently. "Think you ever heard it before?"

There was a long pause before Kirk answered. "Maybe. I dunno. I never paid no attention, Chris."

"Think," Feldhake insisted. "You can't recollect anything more about the man except he was riding a buckskin? Was he fat or thin? Did his voice sound excited or not?"

Kirk shook his head immediately. "I dunno, Chris. He was out in the dark there. There was a light in the carriage-house and I seen the colour of his horse when it shied back into the light. I just figgered it was somebody from town with a message for Ben. I never paid no attention."

A shadow of suspicion crossed Kirk's face. "Why you so anxious to know, Chris?"

Feldhake laughed and reached in his pocket and drew out a gold piece, which he flipped to the man leaning against the door. "You win, Bob," he said easily. To Kirk he said, "Bob's sparkin' the help out there at Combers. He claimed he wasn't out there the night of that party and I claimed he was. But this man wasn't Bob, I reckon—not unless Bob stole a buckskin."

"Hell, why didn't you say so?" Kirk said, grinning. "No, it wasn't Bob. I know that." He turned and Bob opened the door, and Chris waved lazily as Kirk went out into the saddle-room. Bob closed the door behind him. The three of them looked at Feldhake, who was plucking absently at his thick lower lip.

"That's four that said buckskin," Feldhake said presently.

"It was Jimmy Hamp, all right," one of the men said.

Feldhake nodded imperceptibly. "Yes. I reckon so."

Immediately the two men squatting against the grain sacks rose and went out. Bob waited while Feldhake lounged off the sacks to follow them.

"Feldhake," Hardiston said, and Feldhake stopped while he scrambled down the oat sacks and crossed over to face him.

"I've been waiting four days now," Hardiston said. "When do I get the rest of the money?"

Feldhake regarded the little man thoughtfully, frowning. He smiled faintly, shook his head, wheeled and went out past Bob. Hardiston made a sudden gesture to stop him, but checked it and simply stood there while Bob came over and picked up the lantern and headed for the door. Suddenly Bob paused, turned and came back to Hardiston.

"Listen, old man," he said quietly. "You're a little too old to play out a hand like this. If you got sense you'll clear out here, clear out now, right plumb now."

"Why?" Hardiston demanded irritably. "Why? I've got money owing me and I intend to collect it."

"You won't collect any money from him," Bob said patiently. "Don't you see, old man? I'm tryin' to help you. Get out of here before you get him riled."

"But——"

"Sure," Bob said. "Sure. Only you get out. I've seen him shoot a horse for pitchin' with him."

Hardiston stood utterly still a moment, considering this. "Oh," he said then. "You don't think he ever intended to pay the rest of it?"

Bob laughed and went out, and Hardiston stood there in the dark. Suddenly in that room, in that unbearably hot room, he shivered.

Minutes after he left Vannie, Seay was aware that he was riding down this same street, but near the edge of town. He turned up the side street and was immediately in sight of the town with its whirl of people. He felt weary and used up and empty, save for a quiet pity for Vannie Shore. Now that he was away from her, he recalled with grim understanding the passion of her, and the bitterness too. She was a woman who would love a man as she had promised, warmly, and with a quiet depth that would make a man humble beholding it. But not himself. It was all there—the liking for her and the understanding, and even the wanting, but it wouldn't work. He tried to back his intuition by reason, and he found himself puzzled and wordless.

In the stream of the main street's traffic he gave his horse its head and watched the ceaseless milling of this throng with a new wonder. Here, even now, were the honest flat-bed wagons of the immigrants attracted too late by the wild stories of wealth to this camp where every foot of ore-bearing land was at a premium. Sheep among wolves, he thought, as he noticed the bewilderment on the faces of these wagon-drivers. For the quick rough heartiness of the town which was more than confidence, even arrogance, must have been puzzling to these strangers. The long line of freight wagons was as slow and never-ending as it had been for two years now. All this wealth had been taken over and its division settled long since. A substantial part of its men earned the money by hard work, and all the others fed on them, pandered to their vices, and everyone seemed to have fun and money out of it.

There was a tangle of traffic at a four corners that stopped Seay, and while he was waiting impatiently for the stream to move forward, he stood erect in his saddle, trying to see over the crowd.

A man in the street said from beside him, "Jimmy Hamp got it, Phil."

Seay looked down. He didn't know the man, but he had a friendly, work-grimed face.

"He did? Where?"

"In his office."

Seay nodded his thanks and pushed his horse over to the hitch-rail and dismounted. The crowd had clotted around the entrance to Jimmy Hamp's Keno Parlour, but Seay shoved his way through. He was remembering Jimmy's last words to him that night at the Combers', and a slow, steady anger was whipped alive in him. Jimmy had got it. Because he had been discovered warning Seay of the trouble at the tunnel?

Activity in the saloon was at a standstill. Sober men, their girls on their arms, crowded around the office door. A deputy marshal was keeping them out.

Seay slipped past the deputy and entered the office. Jimmy Hamp, his sagging head just under the circle of light thrown off from the table lamp, sat slacked in his swivel-chair, his shirt-front blotted red.

Ferd Yates and Hugh Mathias, called from a poker game at the Union House, were standing near him, listening to the story of a bartender.

Yates glanced carelessly at Seay as he entered, and then his gaze steadied while Seay observed Jimmy Hamp with quiet attentiveness. Then Seay shifted his glance to the smoky window in the side wall. Its pane was broken, shards of glass on the rug below it. Ferd Yates saw that glance and his eyes changed expression a little, flooding a hard alertness into them.

Then Seay nodded to Yates and Hugh.

"How'd it happen?" Seay asked.

Yates said quietly, "You seem to know already, Seay."

Seay raised his careful glance to Yates. "Through the window?"

"That's what you think, isn't it?" Yates said evenly.

"Ferd," Hugh murmured.

Yates said stubbornly, "It took me more than five seconds to figure it out when I come in. It didn't take you that long."

"Maybe that's why you're marshal instead of sheriff," Seay replied quietly.

"Ferd," Hugh repeated.

"You was on one wide woolly prod to-day," Yates said doggedly to Seay. "Maybe you can tell us who shot him."

Seay didn't even bother to shake his head.

Yates continued mildly, "It occurs to me that there was some mention of Jimmy Hamp doin' you a bad turn, and if my memory ain't played out, you claimed Jimmy was in with Chris Feldhake. Wasn't it Chris you was huntin' this morning?"

"Stop it, Ferd," Hugh said quickly. He was cool, immaculate, disinterested, but there was a keyed awareness behind his quick eyes.

"It was," Seay murmured. "I also said something about Jimmy Hamp. What of it?"

In the slaty attention of his eyes, Ferd Yates saw something coming to a head and, stubborn man that he was, did not heed it.

"Then where was you to-night?"

Seay said softly, "Maybe outside that window with a gun in my hand, a knife in my teeth, dynamite in my pocket, blood smeared on my hands, a crippled horse waiting for me in the alley, and seven witnesses with lanterns to watch me."

With an effort of will, Yates repeated, "Where was you?"

Hugh Mathias said reasonably, "That's a fair question, Seay, considering it's asked by a professionally suspicious man." A faint smile raised the corner of his mouth.

" At Vannie Shore's," Seay said.

Yates wheeled, his mouth open to call a deputy, when Hugh put a quick hand on his arm.

" Be quiet now," Hugh rapped out. " If he says he was there, he was. It's easy enough to check on him without calling him a liar."

Yates' mouth closed slowly, but when it was closed it was closed firmly, grimly. Then he said carefully to Seay, " You've made pretty big tracks here for a while, Seay. Just watch out."

Hugh said quickly, " Nonsense, Ferd." He put on his hat and skirted Yates, and took Seay by the arm. " Have a drink with me, Seay."

Seay went out with him. Once on the side-walk, Hugh said, " I meant that. I'd be pleased if you'd have a drink with me."

Seay shook his head. " Some other time. I'm due back at the tunnel."

Hugh nodded, watching the taller man with a kind of ironic curiosity. " You have a gift for bull-headedness," Hugh mused. " Maybe it's what makes you what you are. I wouldn't know, but I think I like it." He jerked his head towards Jimmy Hamp's. " They don't like you here, Seay. That business with Feldhake didn't set well with Ferd. The more he thinks of it, the more he wonders just who was right that night. He doesn't dare ask Feldhake, because he's Janeece's marshal. His conscience absolved you that night, but he was foolish enough to argue with it. I might risk not minding my own business long enough to repeat what he said to you. Watch out."

" Thanks," Seay murmured.

Hugh looked as if he wanted to say more, and Seay waited for him to speak again. Suddenly each saw what the other was thinking, and Hugh chuckled.

" All right," he said, " I'll say it. You weren't by any chance unwise enough to misinform Yates as to your whereabouts to-night, were you? Because he'll check up."

" No. I was at Vannie Shore's."

Hugh nodded, said good-night, and left him. Seay watched him lose himself in that crowd, and immediately his mind leaped to Sharon. Hugh would tell her of Jimmy Hamp's murder, and what followed. He would also mention that Phil Seay, whom Ferd Yates was inclined to suspect, established an alibi with Vannie Shore to help him.

Abruptly, Seay wheeled and swung under the hitch-rack and gathered in the reins of his horse, his irritation making his movements quick and troubled.

Chapter XI

Sharon had made three trips to San Francisco, each time bearing the hard discomforts of stage travel with a resignation that surprised even herself. She had in her bag the last letter from Hugh, which she had got yesterday morning at one of the stage stations. A driver with the coast mail in the boot recognised her, and had delayed the stage long enough to hunt it out and give it to her. Among other things, which she skipped, Hugh had written in his good-humoured, ironic vein that the tunnel was progressing with surprising dispatch. At the tunnel-head they struck diabase ("which, for the benefit of your charming ignorance, I will call a softer rock than hornblende Andesite," he had written), and it seemed that Charles Bonal was at last in luck. At least, he was stretching his tunnel funds further, and the wise and unprejudiced minds in the camp said that, with this progress to show, he stood a chance of obtaining more loans. As it was now, he couldn't hope to finish the tunnel—all he could hope for was hope. There was no mention of Phil Seay in it.

Charles Bonal's letters to his daughter had been kinder. He had not mentioned the tunnel's progress at all, but he had said that he had hauled Seay away from the tunnel last Saturday night long enough for both of them to take too much whisky, after which they watched the last twenty rounds of a prize-fight, that was not so good as many a street brawl he had seen. The absurdity of them doing it made Sharon smile. Prize-fights, she had always believed, were for people of low tastes, or for people like Hugh, who got a vicarious thrill from a brutality they themselves never indulged in. But for Charles Bonal, a street brawler in his past, and Phil Seay, a saloon brawler now, to watch a fight was like a miner prospecting for gold on Sunday.

To be able to laugh at it indicated to Sharon that she had come a long way in these past weeks. When she was in Tronah this last time, she had taken a quiet pleasure in asking her father to recount his early adventures. And Charles Bonal, humouring her, told of his experiences in the rush of '49, and of the terrible fools' rush up the Frazer years later. They were stories touched by the grimness of Charles Bonal's humour, shaded by tragedy and need, and from them she learned of a whole gallery of people who were legend before she was born, and whom her father respected as heroes of a harder day. She was closer to understanding her father then than she had ever been; and curious now, she began to absorb some of his views and much of his wry contempt for these times of swollen greed when money's only gift was the privilege of plundering a land. She listened to his tales of first women in this land, women like Maizie Comber, whose manners might be as rough as files, but who showed a harder learning than manners demand. She did not know that, by learning Charles Bonal's views of times and people, she was preparing herself to understand the views of someone else. Or perhaps she did. Afterwards, when she was alone, she would find herself thinking of a different life, a harder, freer life where a man's work was his badge of honour; and then the shallow, febrile pace of her own made her restive and discontented.

These were the times when she slipped off to San Francisco, hoping old faces and old friends and an escape from the brutal desert heat would supply some interest. And each time she returned to Tronah with a new eagerness, only to find that it, too, had no real place for her. At times, in her confusion, she could not identify the right people with the right places. The men who courted her in San Francisco she expected to meet on the streets of Tronah, and then she recognised the irony of it and laughed at herself, and was suddenly sad and furious. Hugh could not understand her. He was engaged in a silent but none the less deadly fight for control of the Dry Sierras Consolidated, he said. Perhaps these easy, graceful dinners, the occasional parties, the relaxing nights of gambling, were enough for him. Perhaps they took his mind from his cares, but they were not enough for her. They held an implacable boredom for her that Hugh could not understand. She often wondered if Vannie Shore had conquered this boredom in her own sensible way.

But if Hugh understood little of what she was thinking, she understood even less of him. Two weeks ago the hoist cables on the cage of the Dry Sierras main shaft had broken, sending sixteen men plunging thousands of feet to an indescribable death. Hugh had shrugged philosophically and had ordered the man responsible to be dismissed. But Sharon could not help but contrast Hugh's cold sympathy with the hot and savage anger of Phil Seay when nine of his men were threatened with death. Perhaps Hugh would have slaved days and nights without sleep if some of his men could have been saved, but with that new scepticism taken from her father, Sharon doubted it. She knew she was changing, but she had nowhere to turn. The one man who might have helped her with his friendliness she avoided like the plague. And she did not know why.

The night stage let her out at the Union House and she instructed the hotel help as to the disposal of her baggage, then went upstairs. Her father was not expecting her, and she felt a small glow of pleasure as she anticipated the surprise he would show at her return.

She did not knock at his office door, but opened it gently, and the drone of her father's voice coming across the long room was dear and nostalgic.

Bonal must have seen the door open, for his talk ceased, and Sharon opened the door fully. Bonal was rising, a mixture of surprise and delight on his face. He skirted the desk and she was in his arms. The warm smell of cigars and whisky was about him, and she hugged him to her, wordless. After a moment it occurred to her that her father could not have been talking to himself when she opened the door, and that therefore someone else was in the room.

She drew away from her father. In the shadow away from the desk she saw Phil Seay standing before a chair. The tall lean grace of him caught at her throat, and she saw that for this brief moment his rain-grey eyes were not walled away with reserve. Sharon could not explain afterwards why she did it, but she walked across to him and gave him her hand, and then turned to her father, saying, "I hoped it would be this way, Dad."

The quiet pleading in her eyes met puzzlement in Charles Bonal's face for only an instant, and then he chuckled. He said to Seay, "Will we let her in on our stag-party, Phil?"

"I think so," Seay said. Sharon had the courage to look at him then, and his face was friendly, touched with a quiet smile that held no memory of their other meetings.

"I had my mouth open to call Sarita," Bonal said, and immediately proceeded to bawl for the maid. "You wait," he told Sharon mysteriously. When the servant appeared, Bonal said, "Now get this carefully, girl. You're to go down to the kitchen and hunt up Jose. Only Jose will do. Tell him to take those two mallards out of the ice-chest and put them on a plain white platter, a large platter. I won't have any garnish around them. I want three portions of apple chutney placed in side dishes. I want individual salt-cellars, large ones. Also, bring those two bottles of sour, heavy burgundy I picked out this noon. Get silver service, plain white serviettes, and hurry up here with the mess. Now *vamose*!"

Sharon laughed at him. "Does that give me time to scrub the stage road from my face?"

"If you hurry," Bonal said gruffly.

When Sharon had made a hasty toilet she regarded herself in the mirror. Some of the high mountain coolness they had passed through early this morning still seemed to linger on her face. All the weariness of that trip had vanished, and her eyes were bright and laughing.

In the outer room Sarita was laying out the spread on a white cloth. Seay was pulling up chairs.

Sharon was not afraid to be friendly with him now. Her father held up a warning hand as Seay seated her, and Sharon knew that was his signal for silence. Solemnly, expertly, Bonal carved one duck, and then gestured to them to help themselves. They did, while he poured the wine, and then Bonal tasted the duck. First he tasted it and nodded, and Sharon almost giggled. Next he tasted the chutney, raised his eyebrows; and then he passed on solemnly to the salt. He tasted this with all the gravity of a gourmet, and then laughed, and Sharon knew the formalities were over.

Sharon ate and drank with the gusto of genuine hunger, listening to Seay and not speaking often. He lounged back in his chair, one leg thrown over the arm of it, while he and Bonal argued with good-natured violence over the superiority of teal meat to mallard meat. When that argument was settled to nobody's satisfaction, Seay told her of how they both had stolen a day from the tunnel to hunt these ducks up in one of the mountain lakes.

"Wait," Bonal interrupted him, and regarded Sharon with a grave, expressionless face. "I can smell a lie a mile off. He's going to tell you how he shot this big mallard. He lies in his teeth. I shot him." He looked over at Seay. "Weren't you?"

Seay nodded just as gravely. "To the best of my memory, you were blowing mud out of your gun when that mallard rose."

"If I was blowing mud, it was at the mallard—and I hit him," Bonal insisted.

Seay looked at the remaining duck and then casually took his napkin and unfolded it and spread it over the whole duck, covering it completely. Settling back in his chair, his eyes gently mocking but his lean face dead serious, he said, "We'll have a trial. We've got the evidence here—the evidence and a judge."

Bonal studied him shrewdly, then put down his duck leg. "All right. How do you propose to?"

"What load were you using?" Seay asked him.

"Birdshot, of course."

"And I wasn't. I had buckshot loads because that's all Tober could scrape up. That's settled then. You had birdshot, I had buckshot."

Bonal nodded and Seay turned to Sharon.

"Miss Bonal, you unveil the duck. On the stern end of it—towards me—just remove that browned meat on the back. In the clear meat you'll see some small dark holes. That'll be where the shot went in. Dig down and bring out what you find. At least "—he was frowning thoughtfully—" there should be shot there. He was going away from me."

"He was going away from me, too," Bonal said. "That's right."

"He had gone away from you," Seay corrected him. The skin around the corners of Bonal's eyes crinkled with some secret amusement, but he motioned to Sharon. "Get on with it."

The platter was put before Sharon, and while she performed the operation with all the awkwardness of a person who had never held a carving-knife before, Seay and Bonal exchanged amiable insults.

Presently, when they were not watching her, Sharon cried out and held up her two fingers pinched together. Between them was a tiny black ball, and she held her hand midway between them presenting the evidence.

"Whose is it?" she demanded.

First Seay examined it and then his eyes touched hers briefly, and in that look was a secret delighted understanding. He frowned darkly. "That looks a little too small for buckshot," he admitted cautiously.

"Dad, what do you say?"

"Put it over here," Bonal growled. "Let me look at it."

"You'll do no such thing," Seay countered flatly. "He's got his pockets full of birdshot. He'll pretend to drop it, and then substitute evidence."

"I'll hold it right here," Sharon said firmly. "Midway between you."

Bonal leaned over and studied it, and then said exultantly,

"Why, anybody but a plain fool could see that's birdshot. Of course it's birdshot. It's my duck, just as I said."

"Are you sure?" Seay said.

Bonal looked up sharply. "Certainly I'm sure. You never saw buckshot that size, did you?"

Sharon said with sweet gravity, "Then you're certain this is your shot, Dad? This is part of the shot that killed the duck?"

"Dead certain," Bonal growled.

Sharon spread her hand and let the object drop to the white cloth. It was a tiny, black-headed pin, whose shank she had concealed between her fingers, and whose head, unless subjected to a keen scrutiny such as Seay had given it, looked like shot.

"That," Seay mused, "is a new kind of birdshot. What do you call it, Bonal, and where did you get it?"

Sharon looked once at the amazement in Bonal's face, and then she leaned back and laughed delightedly, Seay with her. Bonal looked sheepish, and then roared great laughter and delighted oaths.

That served to cement the intimacy of this evening. Afterwards, Sharon, her wine-glass cupped in her hand, leaned back and listened to these two men. They included her in their talk now, more often than not using her as an audience for the derision of each other's views. Strangely, they talked of the same things, things of which she knew nothing, of the railroad builders of California, of ranch country up in Oregon whose grass was belly deep to a horse, of mining men and mining methods. Once, to prove his point, Seay quoted from the old Spanish of Gamboa, whose commentaries on the origin of mining methods he cited as proof of the beginning of the arrastra method in ore reduction. His Spanish was so fluent that it was seconds before Sharon realised he was speaking it. Before she recovered from her surprise, they were discussing the mystery of copper smelting among the south-western Indians, and each hazarding guesses which the other ridiculed. It was man talk, backed by shrewdness and knowledge, and devoid of the easy graces of conversation, and overlaid with the thrusting of sharp curiosity.

Charles Bonal's black cigars and Seay's pipe filled the room with a thick fragrance, and as the wine mellowed the talk, Sharon began to piece together Seay's history, gleaned in small snatches as he recalled a queer point of construction in the Governor's Palace in Santa Fé, the long sweep of the

Tonto rim, the fish in the gulf of Baja California, the queer pride of the northern Utes and the customs in the timbered vastness of the Canadian Rockies.

Watching his restless face, Sharon thought suddenly of Ben's answer to her question if he knew Seay. "Hell, yes. Who don't?" And she could understand it now, understand that this was a man whom men listened to in these restless times because he talked their talk and had known their yearnings and had not hung back. But always his talk was of places, not himself, and Sharon wondered jealously how much Vannie Shore knew of these things about him which she would never know.

Later, when it came time to go, Seay shook hands with Bonal and then turned to Sharon, the tall easy way of him dominating this room.

"We've forgotten your stage ride must have tired you," he said, half in apology. "I won't do this again."

"But you must," Sharon said eagerly. "I liked it."

His glance held a question that slowly flooded away to give over to that granite reserve, but Sharon sensed that to-night she had won a small victory over him, and one that he would not grudge her.

When he was gone Charles Bonal paced the room with an aimless restlessness that Sharon watched, her back to the door.

Bonal glanced obliquely at her and said, "Shall I send Sarita for Hugh? It's early yet, and he'll be wanting to see you."

"No," Sharon said. "I'd rather not."

She came over to the table and, passing it, put a hand on the back of the chair Seay had just left. She could feel the warmth of his body still in it, and the tiny litter of pipe ashes which he had spilled on the rug was a mute reminder of his presence. Bonal was at the window, looking down on to the thronged street, and he said nothing while the servant cleaned up the table and put the room to rights, and left.

"You're restless to-night, Dad," Sharon said suddenly.

Bonal only grunted, and Sharon came over to him. The street below was a tangle of men and wagons and horses. Off in the night, some shots racketed out, and died, leaving only the war-whoop of some carouser beating the still air.

"Is it the tunnel, Dad?" Sharon asked presently.

He answered quietly, "What makes you think that?"

"You haven't money, and you can't get it. Isn't that it?" Sharon persisted.

Bonal nodded once. "I can get it. But it'll take time. I'll have to make more myself."

"Hugh wrote the drilling was easier now. Isn't there a chance you can put it through before the funds are gone? Hugh said so."

"Hugh," Bonal said without rancour, "is level-headed only in his own affairs. In mine he's an optimist. No, there's no chance."

"Then what will happen?"

"I'll go back to 'Frisco. Give me a few months until I learn all the stock riggings, and I can buy and bribe and threaten and blackmail myself into one of these mine directorates. Give me another few months and I'll have control of it if I don't ruin the mine in the process. If I don't, I can hoard my cut of the loot, and when it's big enough I'll start on the tunnel again." He was quiet a moment. "The only trouble is that by that time this field will be *Borrasca,* played out, the work stopped by water. Then they'll gang up on me and buy me out of the tunnel control—and I won't stand for it."

"How can you stop it?"

Bonal said soberly, quietly, "I can't."

"But it's awful, Dad!" Sharon protested. "You had the idea! You've put it through this far! You mustn't let them step in at the last and let the stupid fools claim the credit!"

"They won't get the credit. Their money will." He sighed. "You see, girl, I have a lot of money from a lot of places. And when my creditors learn that the tunnel work is stopped, this time for good, they'll stampede. Some smart man—more than likely Janeece—will take their shares for a song, and they'll be glad to sell. Then he'll kick me out, put the tunnel through, and all I'll have out of it is the cut of stock I've saved for myself. It——" He shook his head and opened his mouth, and then shook his head again, sighing. "It's just money I'll have, that's all. And I won't give a damn for it then."

"And Phil Seay?"

"What about him?"

"What will he do?"

Bonal chuckled softly. "I've got a notion that he'll cave in every foot of the tunnel on his last day of work."

Sharon was quiet, and presently her father looked over at her. "You like him now, don't you, Sharon?"

Sharon nodded mutely.

"Don't like him too well," Bonal said. He kissed her and said, "I'm tired. I'm going to bed. Good-night."

"Good-night, Dad."

Sharon stood at the window after Bonal had gone, wondering if her face had betrayed her, wondering if it hadn't already, before this. How deep did her father's insight go? He could read men more easily than the printed page, and Sharon trembled a little in that knowledge. For disloyalty was the chiefest crime in Charles Bonal's code, and to-night Sharon had not been loyal to Hugh in thought or deed. But threaded through that fear was a deep, inexplicable happiness that nothing could touch. And Sharon knew, almost sadly, that nothing could destroy it either.

Chapter XII

In the plain room at the rear of the house, which was becoming more and more of a sanctuary, Maizie settled back in the leather chair and regarded the cribbage board. Beulah had just left her hand and gone to mix up some thin claret punch which would help to while away these long hot hours of the afternoon. Maizie closed her eyes and put her head back, the tired lines of her face relaxing a little. Suddenly she opened her eyes and her gaze returned to the cribbage board on the low table facing her chair. She noticed that Beulah had pegged the little ivory counters lightly in the holes, as if in this smothering heat she could not exert herself enough to place them firmly.

A look of wary temptation crossed Maizie's face, but she put her head back again, listening for the faint sounds coming from the kitchen through the door Beulah had left open. Again her eyes opened and strayed to the cribbage board. And then slowly her moccasined foot lifted off the floor, touched the cribbage board and sent it to the floor, where it overturned. Plain satisfaction was written on Maizie's face as she observed that Beulah's pegs were pulled loose, and lying on the rug.

"Beulah!" she called. "Beulah!"

There was a swift scurrying of footsteps and Beulah appeared at the door, a startled look on her broad and homely face.

"I just knocked against the table and tipped the board off," Maizie said impatiently. "Do you remember where you were pegged?"

A look of sly understanding crossed Beulah's face. This accident happened at least twice a week, and she had long since learned with the tact peculiar to a good servant that this was her cue to prevaricate.

"I swear I don't remember," Beulah said. "You've got such a memory, Maizie. You put them back where you think they were." She returned to the kitchen and the punch, knowing that she had thereby sacrificed the game and put Maizie in the best of humours, for Maizie would cheat unashamedly.

The door-pull clanged then, and Beulah dropped her work and hurried out into the corridor. Maizie was at the door of the room and she said gruffly, "You mix that punch. I'll see to it."

Sharon was already in the foyer, and Maizie came up and kissed her. Walking back through the neat house, they chatted together, mostly about the heat.

When they were in the small room again, the cribbage board had disappeared, and the room showed signs of a quick tidying. Sharon leaned her parasol against the wall and sank down into a chair. Maizie regarded her shrewdly for a silent moment, and then said, "Heavens, child. Aren't you used to this heat yet?"

Sharon looked at her without stirring. "Yes. What made you ask?"

"You're peaked. You look like a chicken with the pip."

Sharon only smiled and relaxed.

"How was your trip to the coast? The last one, I mean?" Maizie asked.

"Awful."

Maizie snorted. "Then why did you go?"

Sharon shrugged lazily. Beulah came in with the punch and left, and Maizie served Sharon's glass, which she accepted and sipped listlessly.

"The trouble with young people now," Maizie said shortly, "is that they haven't anything to do. It's the trouble with some old people too, like me," she finshed bluntly.

"What can I do, Maizie?" Sharon asked idly. "If I were poor, I'd have to keep house for my father. But I'm not, so I do nothing."

"Get married," Maizie said.

"You're married. And you complain too."

"I raised four boys and buried three girls," Maizie said grimly. "By the time you do that you won't have to do much more, even though you should."

Sharon said, "But I'm not married, Maizie. I don't even want to be."

"Look at Vannie Shore," Maizie said idly, watching Sharon. She could see her stiffen a little, but there was no other sign of response. "Now she's not married. She works so she hasn't got time to think about marriage."

"Yes," Sharon said.

Maizie squared herself comfortably in her chair, her shrewd old eyes veiled. "Come to think of it, she'll take that in her stride," Maizie went on garrulously. "She's taken everything else—men, one marriage already."

"Yes," Sharon said.

"Queer how attractive she is to men," Maizie mused. "They seem to like her—all of 'em."

"Yes."

"It's that man she used to have that stops them," Maizie said contemptuously. "The fools. They think it's us women that care about a woman being married. We don't give a hang, as long as she doesn't trespass on our property. It's the men that read up on the law and morals, and then give us fits if we break a few, while they bust every one of 'em to their own satisfaction. But when it comes to women—oh, no. They've got to be perfect." Maizie laughed a little. "The fools. Then when it comes to a girl like Vannie, they're stumped by their own rules. Oh well, it serves 'em right, as long as they know what they're missin' and it hurts 'em."

Still nothing but a nod from Sharon. Maizie decided to be bolder.

"Seems like one man might show up in Vannie's life that knew the rules and didn't give a hang," Maizie went on. "From what I hear there's one showing."

Sharon said carefully, "Is there? I can't imagine who."

"Phil Seay," Maizie blurted out.

Sharon's gaze whipped around to Maizie. "Phil Seay? But I thought——" She paused, and the colour began to creep into her pale face.

"What did you think?"

"Nothing. It was just something Hugh told me quite a while ago. About him, Seay, being with Vannie the night a gambler was shot. It—she established his alibi, Hugh said."

"Unh-huh, I heard it too," Maizie said. She sat back and sipped her punch, watching the agitation working in Sharon's face. When Sharon looked over at her again, Maizie was contemplating the far wall.

"Maizie," Sharon said timidly.

Maizie hauled her gaze down.

"Have you—is he—does he still see her?" Sharon asked. "Vannie, I mean."

"What if he does?" Maizie asked curiously. "You don't like him."

"But does he?"

Maizie rubbed her chin and regarded Sharon with a conspiratorial air. "He may. He's going to see more of her if I have anything to say about it." She rose and set her glass on the table. "You know, he won't do anything unless he's rawhided into it, like any other man. I thought of having them over here some night and leaving them alone." Her back was to Sharon and she walked over to the secretaire. Opening it, she drew out an envelope and was careful not to look too sharply at Sharon when she handed it to her, saying, "You know, he's not the roughneck you thought him, Sharon. Read that."

Sharon opened the note. It trembled in her hands.

Dear Mrs. Comber (it read), *I have not thanked you for asking me to that singer's reception. I was called away suddenly, leaving me no time to explain why to you. I apologise, and I did enjoy the company and the rye whisky, what little I tasted of both. Very truly yours.—Phil Seay.*

Before Sharon could comment, Maizie chuckled. "That devil. He's sly too."

"Sly?"

"'I did enjoy the company and rye whisky, what little I tasted of both,'" Maizie quoted. "Isn't that leaving open the way for an invitation for more?"

"I don't think so," Sharon said coldly. "I think it's civil and maybe—maybe impudent, although he meant to be friendly. It's his way."

"It's his way of thanking me for introducing him to Vannie Shore," Maizie said, winking. "I know. He wants me to ask her again some time, and him too, and that's——"

"He does not!" Sharon said sharply.

Maizie's face was carefully surprised. "Why, Sharon," she said slowly. "What are you in such a bother about?"

For one brief second Sharon's defiance was magnificent, and then it crumbled and she jumped out of her chair and rushed to Maizie's open arms and sobbed as if her heart would break. Maizie hugged her, ashamed of the low tricks she had resorted to, but there was yet humour in her eyes.

"I love him, Maizie," Sharon said brokenly. "I—I love him!"

"I know you do, you little fool!" Maizie said. "I knew it from the first time I saw you together. That's why I asked him to my party."

Sharon said brokenly, "But he didn't even see me! He never does! It was Vannie! And—and you did it! On purpose too!"

"Of course I did!" Maizie murmured. "It was one way to break that fool pride of yours by setting another woman on him, an expert!"

Sharon fought her crying, but she kept her face hidden in Maizie's shoulder. "But what will I do?" she moaned. "I've lied, Maizie! I'm—I'm engaged to Hugh."

"Damn him for a tailor's dummy!" Maizie said shortly, and with such violence that Sharon raised a tear-streaked and wondering face to her.

"Send him packing," Maizie said curtly. "Are you going to lose a man, a gid-down, hell-roaring broth of a man, because you're afraid to tell a suit of pressed clothes that he'd better get out!"

"But Dad," Sharon quavered. "I—it's a promise, Maizie, to Hugh. It's loyalty, it's my word, it's——"

"Your word my foot!" Maizie interrupted. "Do you think there's a man alive that counts a woman's word worth a damn until she's dead! Of course not! It's a woman's privilege to lie!"

"But he doesn't love me, Maizie!" Sharon said bleakly, forlornly. "He doesn't love me a bit!"

"He will. He can't help it. He'll fume and——"

Maizie's kindly advice was interrupted by an ear-splitting whoop that racketed through the rooms, rolling echo on echo.

Maizie and Sharon looked at each other, and then Maizie went to the door. The whoop, approaching now, poured into the room with the brassy delight of a madman's.

Ben suddenly appeared in the door. He grabbed Maizie by the upper arms and pulled her into the room in a lunatic dance, and all the time he was yelling, "Oh, god damn! Oh, god damn!"

"Stop that cursing, Ben!" Maizie snorted. "What's the matter?"

"Matter? The tunnel's through!" Ben shouted back at her. "My God, it came out with a rush that washed that drill clean down to the river! It's pourin' water—millions and millions of water! Rivers of water; All the water in the Pintwaters! It's runnin' through that tunnel! It's through!"

For one stunned moment Sharon looked at Maizie with disbelief, and then they were in each other's arms. They were both crying now, and Ben, too happy to be articulate, ran out to tell Beulah, whooping through the rooms again in his lunatic dance.

Fifteen minutes later Ben had the carriage hitched, and he was whipping his horses into a gallop towards town, Sharon and Maizie urging him on. Tronah had taken the news with that good humour which its philosophy reserved for the best man. This morning Charles Bonal had been a fool; now he was a genius. Guns racketed off in the streets, and its traffic was hopelessly jammed with celebrants. Men who had never seen the tunnel, who had sneered at every mention of it, were drinking in the streets. As always, the town took any excuse for a rousing, drunken time.

Ben sawed the carriage at top speed down alleys to avoid the crush. Once out on the road, they found it jammed with people heading for the tunnel and a sight of its miracle. Ben drove through the crowd, scattering them like tenpins. At the top of the pass they could see the whole camp lying below them. Down the millrace, which had been dug so long it was almost a part of the landscape, was a sizeable stream of water, unmistakably water. At the end of the mill-run and over the sides of it were great pools of water, where it had overflowed in the first rush. The camp was boiling with excitement. Growing crowds lined the banks, pouring towards the tunnel. Sharon saw it all in an excitement not far from tears.

At the camp, nobody knew where Bonal was. There was a delirium of joy; nobody talked sense or wanted to talk sense. On the small porch of the bunk-house a huge keg of beer had already been broached, in keeping with Bonal's promise that the night the tunnel was put through, every man could drown in drink if such was his inclination. Smiling, yelling workmen raced through the camp, toting tools or running for those they had forgotten. The townsmen already here were flocking to the tunnel mouth. Even now the water in the mill-run was subsiding, but its flow was steady and continuous.

Sharon directed Ben to go to the office. She got down and ran into it. The first room was empty. She was about to turn away when she remembered the back room.

Opening the door, she saw Charles Bonal seated on the swivel-chair, puffing on the blackest of his cigars, alone. But on his cheeks, clinging to his beard, were tears of unashamed weeping. Without speaking, he took Sharon in his arms. This was the moment he had dreamed about, had fought for and prayed for in his strange way, and now that it was here there were no words to use. They would not come. He clung blindly to Sharon, the force of his hands hurting her.

Later, when he could talk, when they were both calmer, Sharon asked, "But what happened, Dad?"

"Only the Lord knows," Bonal said soberly. "At first we thought we hit a water pocket. We did. Seay was in the tunnel with Hulteen setting off a shot. The shot knocked the plug out. The water rolled at them and they ran. It caught them and washed them out, half drowned Seay and the mucking crew——"

"Hurt?" Sharon said swiftly.

"No. Seay's all right. When the big head of water was past, he went in again to the tunnel. It's his report that makes me certain we're through. The rock formation has changed again. This is a looser gravelly type that almost washes out with the water, but doesn't cave." He looked at his daughter and smiled. "It's the type that Hugh struck before they had to give up work at the bottom of the Dry Sierras shaft."

"Then——"

"It's practically certain we're through—all but the mucking. No drilling, only mucking and timbering. And the water in the Dry Sierras is falling fast. We found that out immediately."

Slowly, then, Sharon got the whole story. The water had picked up the receiving tank and the drill, and rolled them out of the tunnel mouth and part way down the slope. After the great head of water subsided, Seay went in, to return with his report. With agonising uncertainty they had compared notes with Hugh over at the Dry Sierras, had checked the water level in that shaft. It was falling, would be dry by nightfall. It was clear sailing. The Dry Sierras would start digging down, the tunnel mucking forward. Soon, unbelievably soon, the two shafts would meet. Yes, when that happened, the fight was won. The tunnel was finished and timbered then. Janeece would eat crow until he gagged on it. In a few weeks it would be accomplished. Week after that the work on the biggest reduction mill in the Tronah field would start, and it would be erected right on the banks of the Freeling, not a hundred yards from this office. There was more of it, and Sharon laughed at her father's rare loquacity.

When Maizie thought she had waited the proper time she came in and congratulated Bonal. Later, they all started up to the tunnel mouth. As Bonal approached the crowd he was cheered wildly. He was puzzled to find himself regarded now as something of a saint, the saviour of the Tronah field. He could have told them he would be, and had been telling them so for years now, but he accepted their homage without rancour. Workmen who saw him crowded around, and finally, overriding his good-humoured protests, they hoisted him to their shoulders and paraded with him.

Sharon did not get to see the tunnel that day. Separated from her father and surrounded by that rough and riotous mob, she and Maizie went back to the office to wait for him. All of Tronah seemed to be pouring over the hills to the tunnel camp.

An hour later Seay came in, Tober behind him. He stopped short at the door, pleasure overlaying the quiet elation in his face as he saw them. His clothes were almost dry, but he was wet with sweat and his face was runnelling it.

His gaze settled on Sharon, who was smiling happily, and he grinned at her. "Bonal's Bonanza," he laughed. "Do you believe in fairies now?"

Sharon laughed warmly and nodded. "Don't you?"

"How much of this are you responsible for, young man?" Maizie asked.

"Only the drill that made the hole that held the dynamite that blew in Bonanza," Seay said, still laughing. Sharon had never seen his eyes so wild and free, and they almost frightened her.

"Where is Dad?" she asked.

"Six feet off the ground, seated on the shoulders of two Irishmen who won't let him down till dark." For emphasis, the roar of the celebrating crowd poured down from the slope.

Seay asked, "Is your carriage here?" and Maizie nodded.

He turned to Tober and said, "See if you can find it, Reed, and bring it around in back."

"Are we being ordered home?" Maizie asked, after Reed had gone.

For answer, Seay drew her to a window and pointed out. A huge freight wagon with a three-team hitch was just sloping off the higher road down to the camp. All the men who could find a hold were braking its wheels, while the horses fought against them to get it down the slope. The driver, cursing wildly, was snaking his buckskin whip at the revellers. And the cause of it rode high and eloquent on top of the load. The wagon was loaded with beer kegs, and perched on them sat three of the town women, shrieking at their precarious position.

Back of the wagon were several carriages, all loaded down with shrill and already convivial honkatonk girls.

Maizie chuckled at the sight. Sharon, behind her, laughed too, but a little shyly, and Seay turned to look at her.

"In another hour the top will blow off. I've put a dozen sober men to guard the tunnel. All the warehouses are locked." He looked out at the mob now, which was breaking for the beer wagon. "They can't do much more than raze the bunk-houses."

Sharon was a little disgusted with the sight, and she turned away. Tober found Ben and the carriage, and Seay showed them to it.

"We'll have a little party to-night," Sharon told Seay. "Can you come? Just Dad and you and Maizie and Abe and myself." She felt her throat a little tight as she finished, but Seay said only, "Glad to."

But if Sharon hoped for a quiet intimate celebration of their good fortune, she did not get it. No sooner had the five of them sat down to dinner than the maid informed Bonal that neither the office nor the parlour would hold all the callers. Bonal, who knew his west and its ways, left at once. Without him the dinner was pointless. Afterwards, Sharon surrendered the suite, retired to her room and locked her door. And till far beyond midnight, all the friends and acquaintances and a good many strangers called on Bonal to congratulate him and to drink his whisky, and to make this a long night of hilarious revelry. Bonal, tired and exhilarated by all the drinks he acknowledged, laughed in his beard and occasionally looked over at Seay, who was bearing this same treatment with all the tolerance he could muster. Bonal knew who deserved the credit. And he took a grim and boyish delight in watching Seay suffer for success.

Chapter XIII

The meeting was called for evening, and was held in Charles Bonal's suite office. Most of these invited arrived promptly, decorously, and as soon as their hats were taken, were shown into the large room, which now held two large tables set together and flanked by seats for some twenty persons. A buffet loaded with liquors and ice was set against the inside wall. Two hanging kerosene lamps threw light on the table, which was bare save for several ash-trays and two boxes of cigars.

As far as Bonal could tell, they were all here—except Janeece, who was represented, of course, by Ames Herkenhoff, the Pacific Shares manager. It was a strange meeting, and only Hugh Mathias's easy affability saved it from becoming embarrassing.

Seay was fortunate in that he did not know these men, had met less than half of them, and therefore did not hold Charles Bonal's contempt for them. Hugh introduced him, and these mining men regarded him with considerable interest. For weeks now Seay had been driving the tunnel through, day and night, and not once had he left the camp. It was as they had guessed; the drilling was mostly over. All that remained was the mucking and some drilling. The hard part had been the timbering; in some places it had been like trying to tunnel through quicksand. The whole of Tronah had followed the work after the premature announcement of the tunnel's completion, but the luck had held. These mining men had followed it too, ready to admit that Seay was near to finishing a tough job neatly.

Bonal called them to their seats finally, and indicated to Seay to sit on his right. Seay did, covertly regarding the faces of these men around him. When Bonal rose the group became quiet.

Bonal carefully placed his cigar in the tray before him and began to speak. "I won't pretend this is to be a friendly meeting, gentlemen," he announced. "You've fought me too hard for me to hold any affection for you."

There was an uneasy muttering at this introduction.

"I'm privileged to make this announcement in spite of you, so to speak," he went on. "The announcement is no secret to any of you. The Bonal Tunnel is now reality, or soon will be—definitely."

The going was a little easier now, and Bonal picked up his cigar.

"Hugh Mathias, of the Consolidated, tells me that the water in his main shaft has disappeared. Apparently"—and his voice took on an astringent quality—"my predictions were not as wild as you gentlemen were led to suppose."

A square-faced man in his fifties, with the jowls of a bulldog and the twisted hands of a one-time workman, cleared his throat and leaned forward on the table. This was Ames Herkenhoff, of the Pacific Shares.

"We're all eating humble pie, Bonal," he said shortly. "Let's get down to the proposition."

"Good," Bonal said, iron creeping into his voice. "At one time in the history of this tunnel I offered you shares in it and a reasonable proposition for ridding your mines of water. You laughed at it. You won't laugh at this, but you'll take it." He paused, eyeing them with a lazy insolence. "My original proposition was that you pay me two dollars for every ton of your ore that was drained of water by the Bonal Tunnel. My proposition now is exactly double that."

"Nonsense," Herkenhoff blurted out.

"It's no nonsense, Herkenhoff," Bonal said easily. "You'll take it and like it, and I'll tell you why. You'll do it because you can't afford not to. If you don't, you'll hit *borrasca* in another month, and you know it."

Herkenhoff said quietly, "That remains to be seen."

Bonal said in all good humour, "If the rest of you gentlemen persist in sticking to this same absurdity, I'll wait another month until the Pacific Shares, which had a deep shaft, is flooded. Perhaps you'll see the light then."

There was a low murmur of protest. "Go on," someone said.

"I intend to. We'll give Herkenhoff the right to dissent." He looked around the faces watching him. "Maybe we'll get through this sooner if you ask me questions. There's a lot of ground to cover."

Waldman, the Golgotha manager, spoke up, his voice reasonable. "How do you intend to drain all our shafts, Bonal. The water won't seep out."

"I'll cut lateral drifts to them from the tunnel," Bonal answered. "You'll start your own drifts towards me. When we meet your water problem is finished."

"That's expensive," someone objected.

"Who said it wasn't?" Bonal countered quickly. He eyed them steadily, waiting for someone to contradict him, and when they did not, he went on. "Gentlemen, the pumps you are now using will lift water two thousand feet, no more. Most of you are close to two thousand—and the ore gives no sign of pinching out. Is that right?"

They said it was.

"Then provided I can handle the water from your shafts, you can install these same pumps at a depth of two thousand feet—at present, the bottom of your shafts. That will let you take out ore, free of any danger from water, for another two thousand feet. Four thousand in all." He looked around him, and Seay saw the corners of his eyes wrinkle a little, as if he were smiling. "That ought to give you enough profits, gentlemen, to finance a lateral drift to my tunnel."

The company held a non-committal silence.

"That," Bonal reiterated, "is not a matter of choice for you. It's necessity, as I've said before."

He lighted his cigar now and puffed it to life. Seay could see the sardonic delight in Bonal's face. He was enjoying this to the last unrecorded word.

"And now," he said presently, "there's the matter——" He paused and looked at his chair and said to no one in particular, "There's no reason why I can't sit down to this." He did so, and then took up the conversation again. "There's the matter of my reduction mill."

They were watching him again.

"The mill which you gentlemen are going to finance for me," he added smoothly.

He waited until the storm of talk subsided a little, leaning back in his chair and cuddling the cigar in his mouth. Once he winked at Seay, who could not smother his grin of delight.

Suddenly he pounded his flat hand on the table, demanding silence.

"Yes, you'll finance it," he said grimly, "and again it will be because you have to. Do you want to know why? I'll tell you then. It's because any man with a lick of sense—and you've all got that, only you're modest about showing it—can see that it's cheaper to hoist tons of ore a hundred feet, put it in cars, haul it to my tunnel and let it roll out than it is to hoist it twenty-five hundred feet, put it in wagons and haul it five miles. There's the proposition—so simple it's idiotic."

"Why should we finance your mill for you, Bonal?" Bengler, of the Bucko Queen, asked hotly. "It's *your* mill! It's *your* profits!"

"You'll finance it because in the long run it will save you money!" Bonal said shortly. "You'll get your loans back. How can you help it when it's you that will give me my business? And my reduction costs will be a third less than Janeece charges you now. Figures don't lie. The cost of getting the ore to me is negligible. My process is identical to Janeece's. Then why in hell wouldn't you finance my mill and give me your business?" he asked arrogantly. "The more money you save on milling, the more you make on your bullion!"

His words fell on a wrathful silence. Hugh looked over at Seay and shook his head slightly, grinning around his cigar.

"Bonal," someone at the foot of the table said, "it strikes me that we pay you through the nose. You get a cut off every move we make."

"You're damn' right I do," Bonal said grimly. "You're getting off lucky, at that."

Herkenhoff rose and pulled his coat across his barrel chest. "Gentlemen," he said, a wry expression ground into his face. "I, for one, refuse to pay tribute to a robber. Good-night, all."

Bonal chuckled and said, "Anybody else?"

"I'll see this through," someone said. "How do you propose to do this, Bonal? How do you propose to take our ore out?"

"You'll be levied according to the grade of your ore at present and your output," Bonal said. "I'll settle that with you separately. As for my methods, I'll simply haul your ore through the laterals to the tunnel, dump it in cars and shoot it to my mill."

"What about the water, though?"

"The water will run in a channel below the tracks. It's being dug now."

Bonal settled back and peacefully sucked his cigar, his eyes on the faces of these men, taking quiet pleasure in their expressions.

"You've overlooked one thing, Bonal," Waldman said finally. "It's this. You've got to put your laterals through our land. What do you intend to pay us for that right of way?"

"Not a cent," Bonal said cheerfully. "If the laterals don't go through, if you don't help to put them through, matching yard for yard of rock my crew takes out, then you'll cut your own throats. You will have won, but you'll also have bull-headed yourselves into *borrasca*."

He rose slowly and threw his cigar into the ash-tray, and said, "Think it over, gentlemen. There's no hurry. The Dry Sierras is working right now on a dry shaft bottom. It's only a matter of hours before their shaft and my tunnel meet. It's simply a question of how fast the muckers can take the stuff out. To-morrow—next day—come over and see how it works. It really"—his speech was thrusting, dry, cutting—"is so simple that I think you can understand it."

He dismissed them then with a nod that was a little contemptuous.

Chapter XIV

"But this is absurd, Hugh. It's absolutely insane," Sharon murmured.

"Patience," Hugh replied.

They were both standing in the dark alleyway at the side of Dan Stoles' opera house and had been for some minutes. It was a dark well here, casting their voices in hollow echo to the very sky. A segment of the street was visible at the head of the passageway and it was like looking through a peep-hole, like spying. Two men left the sidewalk, stepped into the alley and passed a bottle between them, out of which they both drank, then went their way.

Hugh laughed, and Sharon had the feeling that a murder might easily be committed here without the town discovering it.

"What time did he say he would let you in, Hugh?"

"It's five minutes past that now."

Just then the exit door creaked open and fat Dan Stoles appeared. He held up a warning hand and then greeted Sharon, who nodded indifferently.

"Everything all right, Dan?" Hugh asked.

"I think so. They're calling for the performance now. You'll have to hurry, Mr. Mathias—you and the lady."

"Lead off."

"This is absurd," Sharon repeated, but she stepped in behind Dan Stoles and entered the opera house. They were right by the gallery stairs, and Sharon climbed them impatiently, Hugh at her heels. There was a rhythmic clapping below, which seemed almost to shake the building. Raucous shouts and more raucous laughter rose over the clapping. Dan Stoles led them down a corridor, opened a door, and they were in the smaller corridor on to which the boxes opened. The corridor was deserted. At one of the box doors Dan Stole paused and said to Hugh, "It's dark in there, Mr. Mathias. You said no lights, remember."

"That's right." Hugh slipped him a gold piece and then opened the door, and he and Sharon slid inside. The house was dark, the curtain still lowered, and it was with difficulty that Sharon found a chair.

When they were seated, she said, "These are wretched seats, Hugh."

"Did you want to be seen?" Hugh countered.

Sharon did not have time to reply before a man stepped out from the wings and raised both hands. He had the flashy, arrogant air of a professional entertainer, or a gambler, and he could not command silence for some minutes.

"Gentlemen," he began—and was roundly hissed. He laughed. Sharon looked bored.

"Men of Tronah," he shouted. There was wild applause. It rose wave on wave from the whisky-sodden air.

"Men of Tronah," he said again. "The first number on this evening's olio will be Miss Margie Borden, the peerless——"

He could get no further. A mighty roar of protest went up from the audience below. They hissed and booed and jeered and shouted for a full minute, until the master of ceremonies raised his hands to command silence again.

"I am in the wrong, gentlemen," he announced. "The first number on the evening's olio will be the main attraction. Mr. Buck Hanighen, of Winnemucca and points north, will pit his bulldog against the wild cat owned by Shagnasty Will Curbin, of local fame."

A shout of applause drowned out the rest of his speech, and he subsided, waiting until there was comparative silence again.

"The fight will be to the finish, gentlemen. There is a hundred-dollar side bet as a prize between the owners of the principals. Place your bets, gentlemen!" he shouted, and lowered his arms and went into one of the wings. His advice was unnecessary. Bets had been made for the past week, and the prospect of this bloody fight to the finish had been so well advertised that seats to-night were at a premium.

There was a preliminary shiver of the curtain before it sailed up, revealing a stage bare except for a huge chicken-wire pen some ten feet high.

There was more applause, and then the audience started to stamp and clap.

Mr. Buck Hanighen was first on the stage, and he was pulled on to it by a bulldog on the end of a leash. The dog was a squat, head-heavy brindle bull with a monstrously ugly head and face so scarred it was laughable. Nose glued to the floor, bowed legs almost straight behind him with the exertion of pulling his master, he followed some invisible trail with implacable relish until he came to the footlights. The roar of the crowd made him look up, and eyed it briefly with a good-natured cynicism before he resumed his sniffing. Master Buck Hanighen touched his derby hat and grinned.

When Shagnasty Will Durbin entered with his protégé there was a wild yelling. Shagnasty, bald as rock and perspiring freely, had a good-sized wild-cat by the scruff of the neck, and he lugged it in like a satchel, spitting and yowling and helpless, for its feet were strapped together. The bulldog showed no interest at first, but when Shagnasty Will approached the footlights, the bulldog woke up. He gave one savage lunge, which almost pulled his master's arm from its socket, and Shagnasty Will Durbin retreated.

It took two men inside the ring to hold down the wild-cat while Shagnasty unstrapped its feet. Then the dog was lifted in and held by two more men. At a given signal the dog was unleashed, the cat freed, and the four men dived for the gate of the ring.

Sharon gave a tiny cry of concern, and Hugh laughed.

There had never been any doubt in the bulldog's mind as to his purpose here, but there was evidently some in the mind of the cat. Ears flat back on its head, eyes wide and mouth wider, it bounded to one side and the dog crashed into the gate, its legs working furiously on the slippery stage floor to check its momentum. And then came the rout. The cat ran round and round the circle, a great tawny streak of motion, the bulldog lunging vainly for its hindquarters, and crashing into the wire-netting. The miners roared with delight at the sight.

At one of the collisions with the wire, the flimsy gate gave way, but no one seemed to notice it. Suddenly the cat did. It bounded through the gate and paused for one brief second, while the bulldog proceeded to try to batter the cage down in snarling fury.

There was a sudden silence in the house.

Someone yelled, "Shagnasty, get that damned thing!"

Then the cat moved. In one bound it cleared the footlights and landed on top of the piano in the orchestra pit. The dog by this time had stopped his assault on the wire, and had got outside the cage by tracking the cat. Nose to the boards, he ran after her, crossed the footlights and tumbled off the stage. A crash among the orchestra chairs was plainly audible.

And then pandemonium broke loose as the men in the first row realised that the scene of the fight would very likely be transferred to their laps.

Sharon, eyes wide with excitement, half rose in her seat.

"Hugh, they're both loose!" she cried, but Hugh was at the edge of the box, looking down.

Nothing is more contagious than panic, even good-natured panic. There was a wild scramble in the front rows for the protection of the rear, and in less than thirty seconds complete pandemonium let loose.

A howling, shouting, laughing, fighting mob was clawing its way to the exits. Four men peered over the footlights, waving their arms frantically, while the bulldog, in a fury of frustration, was trying to climb up the piano to get at the cat. The cat stood this for a moment, then lazily leaped clear of the orchestra pit to land on the row of seats. Then crazily, slipping and falling, it picked its way across the now empty seats to one of the gallery pillars, and started to climb it. The dog was hot after it, its savage snarls filling the house with terrible sound.

"Hugh!" Sharon cried. "We've got to get out of here."

Hugh was already pulling Sharon's chair out of the way. "Easy, darling. They're both on the other side."

Sharon ran out into the corridor, and Hugh strode behind her. At the stairs the whole gallery was draining down to the main floor, and soon Sharon was in this jostling, riotous mob. Somehow, Hugh managed to wedge himself between her and the crowd, and the very panicked momentum of the mob carried them downstairs and out the side exit. Once on the street, Sharon, dishevelled, breathless and frightened, took hold of Hugh's arm and let him lead her across the street and to the hotel.

Once in the parlour, Sharon sank down in a chair and stared at Hugh. Hugh's face showed first concern, and then faint amusement, and then he burst into laughter. Sharon's eyes danced with cold anger as she watched him, but Hugh could not restrain himself.

"Hugh!" Sharon said angrily, stamping her foot. "Stop that!"

Hugh subsided gradually and drew out his handkerchief and wiped the tears from his eyes, while Sharon looked on coldly.

"I'm sorry, darling," Hugh said faintly. "The combination was too much."

"Is a person's genuine fright a laughing matter to you?" Sharon demanded icily.

"Not at all," Hugh said soberly. "It was—well everything, the whole ridiculous thing."

"If you knew it would be ridiculous, why did you insist that I go?" Sharon asked hotly.

"I'm sorry," Hugh said apologetically.

"But why did you, Hugh?" Sharon persisted. She knew she was being unreasonable, but then she felt an unreasonable anger, an anger that was as hot as it was humiliating.

Hugh's face changed subtly and he reached in his breast pocket for a cigar. "Now calm down, dear," he said soberly, almost warningly. "The whole affair is over, and I'm very sorry I dragged you to it. I thought it would amuse you."

"Since when has the spectacle of two animals tearing each other to shreds amused me?" Sharon said coldly.

"All right, it never has," Hugh said, a little edge to his voice. For a moment they stared at each other, Sharon with a quiet malevolence that amazed Hugh. Slowly he laid down his unlighted cigar and rose and came across to her. Facing her, he spread his legs, and put his hands on his hips.

"In heaven's name, Sharon, what has got into you lately?" he asked with quiet urgency. "You were looking at me then as if you hated me."

Sharon only shook her head and bit her lip.

"It's my turn to ask questions now," Hugh said. "I repeat, what has got into you?"

"The devil of doubt," Sharon murmured, almost inaudibly.

"What did you say?" Hugh asked, bending over a little.

"Nothing. I don't know."

"Nor do I. Nothing I do seems to please you any more. You—you aren't the same."

"How not the same, Hugh?" Sharon asked softly.

Hugh hesitated, wondering if he detected a note of flippancy in her voice. He decided he didn't; Sharon was never flippant in serious moments, and this was a serious moment.

"Why—it used to be easy to amuse you, Sharon. We liked the same things, enjoyed the same people, went the same places and had a good time." He laughed shortly. "Lord knows, this camp is dull enough for a woman. But you've money, darling. You've the same sort of friends you're used to. You have comforts. You have——"

"Maybe that's just the trouble, Hugh," Sharon put in quietly.

Hugh frowned. "I don't understand. What more could you want?"

"Oh, nothing," Sharon sighed. "I—I've changed, Hugh. I don't think the end and aim of life is to be amused any more, that's all. Everything is the same; I'm different."

"But why?"

"I can't think it's a virtue to be idle, Hugh. I can't see the holiness of having a lot of money. I don't think a man is a swine because he wears a soiled shirt. I don't think people who sleep at night instead of playing are dull and somehow vicious." She raised her hands in a gesture of inarticulate and unknowing pleading. "This isn't the real thing, Hugh. I'm on a bridge looking down at the water. I'm dry and comfortable, but I have a terrible longing to swim."

"Then swim."

"I can't."

Hugh said dryly, "If I smelled of sweat when I called every night, if I left at ten because I need sleep to work; if my hands were horny with callouses; if I resented the good fortune of other people and cursed them, would it make you admire me more, Sharon?"

"Yes!" Sharon said quickly, with such violence that she surprised even herself. "None of those things are virtues in themselves, Hugh, but they point to one thing. That the man who has them is human! Even the resentment at good fortune! Envy is human. You haven't it! Sweat is vulgar, and it's human too, Hugh. Weariness is human. Discouragement is human. Lust and cruelty and foolishness and brawling and cowardice and bravery are all human, Hugh. And you are without them."

Hugh's face flushed. "I'm greedy enough to want ten million dollars for you, Sharon. I lust enough so I want you terribly. I'm cruel enough to use every method I can to get on top. I'm coward enough to be afraid of a street brawl. And I'm brave enough to admit this all to you, Sharon. Am I not human enough now?"

Sharon had one impulsive moment of affection for him, a moment which she fought with all her will. She wanted to kiss him and make up, to be safe in his arms, safer in the knowledge that he loved her. But a wild and untameable hope stirred within her, and she instinctively knew that this was too easy, and because it was, it was also cheap.

She shook her head gently. "No, Hugh. Don't ask me why. You—you just aren't."

Hugh's anger was gone. He said gently, "To-night, Sharon, I was going to remind you of a promise. Do you remember? You must have been expecting it. Don't you remember what I was pledged to ask when the tunnel went through?"

"Yes," Sharon said in a small voice. "You were going to ask me to set the date for our wedding."

"Yes." Hugh looked steadily at her, and Sharon had no answer for him. He turned away and went over to the table and picked up his cigar, and dropped it again. Then he said, without turning around, "Is there someone else, Sharon?"

"Who could there be?" Sharon asked wearily.

Hugh pivoted on one heel to face her. "The only man I know who meets those requirements is a man you know too, Sharon. He brawls, and he's cruel and he's—he's human enough, God knows." He paused. "It's Phil Seay."

Sharon felt her pulse quicken at the mention of that name, but she was not afraid to hear it. She regarded Hugh levelly, silent.

"Is it Phil Seay?" Hugh asked relentlessly, doubt in his eyes.

"He fits that description," Sharon said steadily. "Because he does, he hates me, I think. He wouldn't acquire me because he's through playing with toys—if he ever did."

"Sharon!"

Sharon rose, making a weary gesture with her hands. "Leave me alone, Hugh. All I've told you is the truth. But I'm confused."

Silently Hugh picked up his hat. "Perhaps this is ruthless," he said in a low voice. "I—I've got to be ruthless, Sharon. Will you marry me?"

"I don't know!" Sharon cried, her voice tormented.

"Good-night, my dear."

"Good-night, Hugh."

When he was gone, Sharon went to her own room, and immediately hated it and came back to her father's office. The rank fragrance of his black cigars seemed to have washed the room with Charles Bonal's own peculiar smell. Sharon sat down in one of the deep leather chairs and closed her eyes. She had told Hugh as much as she knew herself—except, of course, that she loved Phil Seay. Was that any of Hugh's business? Could he even understand it, much less forgive it? How transparent she must be, to have Hugh settle on the name so easily, so obviously. Suddenly she did not care. She had told only the truth—or three-quarters of the truth. Long ago she had given him her word, and some fine-grained honesty that Charles Bonal's daughter could not help but have would not let her break that promise. But if Hugh knew that she didn't love him, couldn't admire him, would he even want her to keep that promise? Sharon hoped not, but she remembered

Hugh's stubborn question just before he left. For one frightened moment she realised that this question was a portent, a sign that Hugh might hold her to that promise. The thought was suddenly unbearable.

She heard the door open and Charles Bonal came in. She waved to him, and he crossed the room to her. His eyes were shining, and approaching, he stopped to brush the layered dust from his trousers. He chuckled a little, too, half to himself.

"What've you been doing, Dad?"

"I was over with Phil at the tunnel, watching them push it through."

"It's through, then, Dad?"

"Absolutely. To-morrow will see the last timbers in."

Sharon looked down at his dusty clothes. "But the dust. That isn't mud."

Bonal laughed again. "I sent the buggy on ahead and drove a freight-team home." Shaking his head with pleasure, he went on, "Your old man isn't a cripple yet. But, my God, that's a job without a roughlock."

Going over to the taboret, he took out a bottle of whisky and poured himself a drink. His eyes were still shining with the elation of this night as he sat down. "Hugh gone?" he asked, and when Sharon nodded, he said, "Sort of early for him, isn't it?"

"I sent him, Dad."

Bonal looked up at her and then away. "Spat, eh?"

Sharon didn't answer him. Instead, she said, "What's your opinion of a person who'll break his promise, Dad?"

"What did Hugh promise you that he didn't give you?"

"You didn't answer my question."

Bonal's veiled eyes studied her for a moment and then shrewdness crept into them. "Depends," he said slowly. "In a business proposition he'll sink himself sooner or later. In a personal one he won't be trusted. In an affair of the heart, I dunno."

"Why don't you?"

"Depends," Bonal hedged. "If a man is held to all the nonsense he tells a woman, he'd likely wring her neck some night." He sipped his whisky thoughtfully and then said, "And, contrariwise."

"Then it works both ways?"

"My dear girl," Bonal said bluntly, "if you're asking for my advice and it has to do with Hugh, you won't get it."

"Did I ask?" Sharon flared up, and then laughed.

"No. And you'd better not. I don't know anything about love," Bonal went on. "When your mother and I were married, it wasn't discussed—or not to the degree it is to-day. I was a young fella gettin' ahead and she took a shine to me. She was a pretty thing, with lots of common sense and a sense of humour. We liked each other's company, so we got married." He paused thoughtfully. "It worked out all right. Fine."

When Sharon didn't say anything, he asked from around his drink, "That help you?"

"Not much," Sharon said quietly. "I'm not sure I want to marry Hugh, Dad." If she thought this would startle her father, it did not. He raised one of his black eyebrows, nodded and took another sip of his whisky. "All right."

"But I promised him."

Bonal smiled meagrely in his beard. "Years ago—back in Illinois, it was—I went to a camp meeting," he began. "They had a good preacher there, one of these hell-fire boys. This meetin' was to fight the evil of liquor. After the third day of it, he got me, and I took the pledge." He set down his glass. "I was eleven at the time. How could I tell I'd change my mind? I did though." He added dryly, "I've never thought it necessary to write that estimable gentleman to tell him I renegged."

He got up, finished his whisky, and whistling faintly, went into his room, leaving Sharon as confused as he had found her.

Chapter XV

Seay was umpiring one of the interminable arguments between Borg Hulteen and Reed Tober. The three of them were standing at the junction of the Dry Sierras Consolidated shaft and the Bonal Tunnel. The full-timbered walls were seeping water, which runnelled down to the floor and flowed sluggishly away, collecting in small pools. The air was cooler now there was a draft of air that flowed through the tunnel and up the shaft. It was so strong that the lanterns overhead swung unsteadily, their flames guttering. It was a cleaner air, too, freed of all the fetid smells of weeks ago.

Clumping over to a wall, he squatted, bracing his back against it, and contemplated the finished job. The drone of Borg's profanity faded a little. His feet felt hot in the rubber boots, but he looked around him with a grim feeling of pride. This was his job, his work, and he had put it through.

Tober turned to him and then jerked his head towards Borg. "When is this ape goin' to start drillin' again?"

Seay shook his head. He couldn't hear above the thin cascades of water that were falling down the Dry Sierras shaft and joining to make a small stream that ran down the tunnel floor. Ten years from now, Seay was thinking, there may be a big pump where we are standing, and the Dry Sierras shaft will drop off here to another two thousand feet of depth. Millions of dollars, thousands of tons of ore would travel that shaft, would be dragged down this tunnel, and all because Charles Bonal was a man of vision and unconquerable.

He rose and turned to the pair of them, still arguing, and took Reed by the arm. "Come on. Put it in a drawer until you can hear each other."

Borg stopped his cursing and grinned. The three of them went back to the dump car, climbed on, and Borg whipped up the mule. The long haul out was not dull to Seay. Every foot of this represented blood and bone and muscle, and sacrifice and cunning and stubbornness. The lanterns at intervals threw twisted shadows on the wet walls of the tunnel side. They would plunge into its feeble circle of light and then dive into darkness again, the pinpoints of light ahead stretching in a long row. Only the lantern rigged on the mule's collar gave a steady light, and it bobbed and twisted and flickered.

Soon they came to the work crew, which was digging the deep trench in the floor of the tunnel. Here the water drained from the mines would flow under the tracks on which the ore cars would be hauled. It was easy work now compared to the tunnel drilling, and upon its completion, the tunnel would be ready to operate.

Outside, the attention of the camp seemed turned away from the tunnel. The foundations of the reduction mill were being put in. The slapping of the doublejacks of the workmen filled the hot afternoon air with sound and fury. Already the trenches were dug in orderly rows, lipped with the rock and dirt taken from them. Soon now, Seay thought, Bonal would not need him any more, and then he would drift.

He swung off the car and looked off towards the office. A saddled horse stood hipshot in its shade. One of the guards, who paced the tunnel mouth night and day after the cave-in, nodded to him, and Seay tramped down the slope.

In his office Vannie was seated in his swivel-chair, her

booted feet on his desk. She was wearing a pair of miner's dungarees and a khaki shirt open at the neck, and her face had the pleasant freshness of activity.

"I took another look at your tunnel," Vannie said. "It looks like the Dry Sierras water trouble is over."

"For good," Seay said. He sat down and pulled off his rubber boots, and then, still barefooted, he reached in his pocket and brought out his pipe, and packed and lighted it. Vannie watched him, tenderness and pride in her eyes.

"You carry your luck with you, don't you, Phil?"

Seay laughed. "That luck was Bonal's."

"No. It was yours. Why not admit it? Bonal, with all his hard-headedness, couldn't have pushed the tunnel through."

Seay shrugged and pulled on his leather boots. The even heat poured in the windows, merciless in its pressing insistence, yet Vannie seemed cool and pleasant, and only slightly dishevelled. A streak of dirt across her chin showed dark on her golden skin, and Seay touched it with his finger. "You didn't go into the tunnel far enough. There's water enough in there to wash with."

Vannie scrubbed at her chin. "I practically had to kiss the guards to get close enough to look into it."

Seay regarded her fondly and then laughed, and sat down on the desk.

"Come to borrow back your track?" Seay asked.

Vannie shook her head and did not smile. "I came to ask questions, Phil."

"Like what?"

Vannie didn't answer immediately, but instead took her feet off the table and leaned back in the chair and gazed thoughtfully out the window.

"How many mines have signed up with Bonal yet?" she asked presently.

"Three-four. Why?"

"Why haven't the others?" Vannie asked slowly.

"Some men take a lot of licking."

"Just that?" Vannie asked, turning to regard him. "When it's inevitable, why do they hold back?"

"Let Bonal worry about that," Seay told her. "But he's not worrying. Why should he?"

"That's just the trouble," Vannie murmured. "He's not worrying enough."

Seay scowled. "How do you mean?"

Vannie's deep, steady gaze settled on Seay, a long moment, and then she laughed abruptly, softly. "You'll laugh at me, Phil."

"About what?"

"I don't know. It's nothing I can pin down. Only, something's underfoot around here, among these mines. It's something they don't want me to know about, because I've always been for Bonal, have helped him."

"What is it you've seen?"

"Well, to-day I went over to see Benger at the Bucko Queen. He's my next-door neighbour, you know. We've been fighting over our boundary for a couple of months, and Benger got Judge Baily to clap an injunction on me ordering me to quit work in one gallery that was close to the boundary."

"What about it?"

"This morning was the morning set for Judge Baily to hear the arguments. The hearing was to be held at the Bucko Queen, so the court would be close to the ground in dispute. Baily wasn't there."

"Why not?"

"When I got there, Benger showed me a note from Judge Baily saying that the hearing must be postponed because he had to leave town for an indefinite stay."

"What of that?" Seay asked.

"Nothing. Only when I went over to the Bucko Queen with Waldman, my manager, I thought I recognised four rigs tied outside the office. They belonged to Forsythe over at the Southern Union Mills, at the Petersburg, Trout at the Bismarck, and Herkenhoff."

"A meeting, then?" Seay asked.

"When I came out the teams were gone—as if somebody had left them there by mistake and had hoped I hadn't seen them."

Seay sucked on his pipe. "Well, what's the matter with that? Can't a bunch of thieves talk business?"

"But two of those three men never liked each other much," Vannie pointed out. "Why the friendship? And with Benger?"

Seay shrugged. "All right, why?"

"I don't know. There's only one thing that would bring all those men together. Tunnel talk."

"And why shouldn't it?"

"But why didn't they want me to know it?" Vannie asked. "When I saw Benger he looked as if he'd just stepped on a little chicken. He wouldn't let me in his office and he hurried me out."

Seay laughed at her, and Vannie smiled back, but there was still a look of concern on her face.

"All right, Vannie, who could happen?" he asked her. "They've only got to take Bonal's proposition or leave it—and they'll take it later if they don't now."

Vannie shook her head. "It looks queer, Phil. Then, too, Baily is gone. If they tried to do something, where would the court come from that would stop them?"

"Something like what?"

Vannie shrugged. "I said you'd laugh at me, Phil. Still, I can't help feeling uneasy. These men haven't signed Bonal's agreement. Maybe they don't intend to."

Seay lounged off the desk and walked over to his coat, and brought out some tobacco. "You're spooky, Vannie. Go back and keep your ears open, and I'll see you again."

"When?" Vannie said swiftly.

"To-morrow night. I'll come over. I don't——" Some queer expression on Vannie's face made him pause. "What's the matter?" he asked.

Vannie was smiling in all her loveliness. "I didn't think I'd ever hear you say that again, Phil," she murmured.

"Say what?"

"That you'd come over to see me."

Impatience crept into Seay's eyes. He pocketed his pipe and came over to face her. "Vannie, I'll come and see you any time I want to, if you want me. But the other—like that night—it's no go. Clean done. You understand that, Vannie?"

She nodded humbly. "Then come over to-night. I haven't said all I wanted."

"I can't. I—I've got an engagement," Seay said. Vannie looked at him so steadily that he felt the colour creeping up his neck.

"Oh," Vannie said quietly, then, "Sharon?"

"Yes. Miss Bonal."

Vannie smiled enigmatically. "It's still 'Miss Bonal.'" She shrugged and walked slowly past Seay. "You hate me for what I said about her that night, Phil?" she asked, her back to him.

"I think you were wrong, that's all."

Vannie sighed. "Well, that's all you need to think. Good-bye, Phil. To-morrow night, then."

Seay watched her mount and ride off, an erect proud woman.

Back at his work over the plans of the reduction mill, he found it hard to concentrate.

It was six when he emerged from the barber shop, freshly shaven and bathed. His boots were polished dully, and his grey trousers were tucked into their tops. His coat was loose, comfortable, his shirt open, and when he mounted the stairs to Bonal's suite he patted his pocket to make sure he had brought his pipe.

Sharon was waiting for him in Bonal's office, and she rose and crossed to him and shook hands with him. Then she stepped back and pulled out the skirt of her dress of net over shimmering satin.

"You said at six, and I've been ready ten minutes. And you said something simple. Is this simple enough?"

She read the look of consternation in Seay's eyes, and she said quickly, "Oh, it isn't, is it?"

Without making him answer, she turned and said over her shoulder, "I'll change. And I'll hurry too."

When she came back only a minute later, she was wearing a pink lawn dress, demure with its long sleeves and high collar.

Seay said, "I like that."

"It's not too—too——"

"Grand? No. Come along."

When they reached the sidewalk, Seay said, "We'll walk. It's only a short ways. A buggy would frighten them."

Sharon nodded eagerly. This was a new experience for her. Two nights ago, when, in the presence of Seay and her father, she had expressed boredom with the routine of her day, Seay had made a strange offer. She had listened to it with quickening heart, and had accepted his invitation promptly. He knew, he said, a place that had never known boredom, people who would not recognise it. Would she care to have supper with them? They were simple people, shy of elegant strangers, but good people, working people.

Now, putting her arm through his, she felt a good kind of excitement, one that she had not known since she was a little girl. Occasionally she looked up at Seay, whose long strides she was hard put to match. His face was reserved, uncommunicative, but she did not feel the need of speech either. The evening jam was just beginning to swell through the streets, but Seay piloted her through the crowd without ever bumping her. Almost, it seemed, men and women gave way to him.

Certainly he seemed to know many of these people, most of them rough-looking characters. Invariably his greeting was the same—a curt nod, a trace of a smile, and a low-voiced, "Howdy, Ed," or Bill, or Jim. The men in turn returned his greeting and tipped their hats respectfully. She had never had this feeling before of being with a person who counted for something among a strange, rough people. Hugh and her father spoke mostly to the men in stiff hats and derbies who hung around the hotel.

Clear of the business section, they turned up a side street which had a neat board-walk. The houses were not grand, neither were they shabby. The few flowers in the windows or at the edges of the gravelled tiny yards gave it a cheerful air. It was obviously a row of workers' homes, but it had a kind of pride, too, that Sharon did not miss. The children playing in the street looked well fed and happy, if dirty, and their greetings were polite and a little shy. Seay looked obliquely at her to see how she was taking this, and he could see only interest in her face.

At a tiny stone house surrounded by an iron fence, Seay opened the gate and piloted her through it. They walked up the steps in a leisurely way, and as they were on the porch, Borg Hulteen appeared in the door.

He was grinning, his face scrubbed and shining, his shirt clean.

"Hallo, Phil," he boomed, and then his gaze fell on Sharon. For one brief moment his honest, bony face reflected a quiet amazement and his glance whipped to Seay. And then, like any man unashamed of himself and his possessions, and welcoming a stranger, he smiled at Sharon.

"Miss Bonal, this is Borg Hulteen."

Sharon put out a tentative hand and Borg took it. When she smiled at him Borg was won over. He led the way back through the house, avoiding the parlour as if he had not seen it, and marched straight to the kitchen. A bracket lamp was lit against the coming dusk, and by its light they could see a woman sitting in a chair, undressing a small boy. Beside the woman, a little girl of five, utterly naked, was regarding their entrance with wide-eyed astonishment.

But it was the woman Sharon noticed. She gave a little cry of delight, rose, slinging the boy on her hip, and came over and kissed Seay with a resounding smack.

"Hallo, Kristin," Seay said smiling, and turned to Sharon. "Kristin, this is Sharon Bonal," Seay said.

Borg's wife gave Sharon her hand. She was a big, full-breasted woman, just out of girlhood, with the smoothest skin and the palest blue eyes Sharon had ever seen. There was a flush to her face, and her eyes were bright with excitement, and if Sharon expected the name of Bonal to impress her, she was disappointed. Her smile was warm and friendly, her glance anything but critically appraising. Immediately, Sharon felt, she was accepted. The child on Kristin's hip squirmed and made a noise, and Kristin laughed.

"Heavens, I'd forgotten Karl." She set him down on the floor and he ran to his sister. Together, both as naked as the day they were born, they stood hand in hand regarding the strangers.

Sharon laughed with joy at the sight, and Kristin said, "You scoot to bed, you two. And Sigrid, don't forget to make Karl say his prayers."

This was the introduction, then, Sharon thought, and she could feel Seay's inquisitive glance upon her.

The smell of cooking in the big kitchen was delicious, and of strange foods that Sharon could not name. In less than a minute Kristin had her by the stove, and while Sharon listened to the talk about the children, she looked at the room. This, too, was strange. The walls seemed to be built of hewn timbers, and in a far corner, away from the heat of the stove, was one of the most massive tables Sharon had ever seen. It fitted against the wall, which held the same heavy benches. The edges of the table and benches were carved, Sharon could see. Above the benches were designs scrolled in the timbers of the wall, and painted with gay colours. Between every design was a clean polished tile, blue and white. The table was already set, and with a heavy silver, and rich linen that glowed warmly in the light of a candelabra loaded with fat candles.

Sharon was immediately pressed into service putting the food on the table, and there was so much of it that she wondered how the stove could have cooked it all.

When Kristin had put off her apron she came to the table and they seated themselves. Sharon was on the bench, her back to the wall, and next to Seay. There was a small glass of brown fiery liquor at each place which, when once down, seemed to kindle the appetite until hunger was almost unbearable.

"You like that, Miss Bonal?" Borg asked, indicating the liquor.

Sharon nodded. "It's strong, but it makes me hungrier. What is it? Something Scandinavian?"

Borg threw back his head and laughed. "That's bourbon whisky," he said. "It takes a Swede to teach an American how to drink his own liquor."

The food was a revelation to Sharon. There were Swedish dishes—*getmesost, knakkebrod,* and rosetest, small fried pies filled with jam.

All of it was strange and good, and Kristin blushed with pleasure when Sharon complimented it. Kristin told Sharon a little of her life here, how Borg had tried to fix over part of the house to look like their homes back in Wisconsin, which, in turn, were built on the order of the old-country places. It was foolish, really, Kristin said, because they would be moving again soon. When coffee was served it was thick and strong, and Sharon needed its strength to keep her from settling back into the amiable stupor that comes from over-eating good things. Seay paid little attention her, and Sharon thought she knew why. He had put her on her own among these people, seeing if she could win their friendship.

It was true. Seay listened with half an ear to the women talk, while Borg talked of anything that came into his head. There was none of the profane, hard-fisted workman about Borg now; he was easy and friendly and gentle. When it came time to clear the dishes, Seay saw Sharon rise immediately to help. The two women were chattering away, oblivious to the men.

Later, Borg got out his accordion, and they sat around the table and listened to him play. His stubby calloused fingers held a kind of magic in them that turned the accordion into a full-throated organ. He played half a hundred of the Scandinavian folk-songs, bits of opera, folk-dances. Sometimes Kristin, recognising a tune as an old favourite, would rise and show Sharon the steps to the old country dances. There was a pitcher of wine on the table and a bowl of nuts, things as simple and good as the music.

But as it grew later, Seay felt a depression settling on him. He watched Sharon covertly, and his face settled into a gravity that seemed strange in all this gaiety.

Soon, then, he rose abruptly and said they must leave. Sharon wanted to protest, but what she saw in Seay's face stopped her. Kristin and Borg both protested politely, but Seay was firm. Borg was a working man and had to get sleep, he said.

At parting, Sharon and Kristin kissed each other. Seay could tell that Borg and his wife liked her, and that the evening had been fun for them all.

Once out in the night, Sharon took Seay's arm and they walked slowly towards town. The night sounds away from the business of town were remote and individual. The stamp mills were hammering the high night sky with their pounding, a kind of sustaining chorus that was the background of the town.

Sharon was first to speak. "I had a lovely time," she murmured. "I didn't know such simple things could be so much fun. And how nice they were to me."

"They liked you," Seay said.

Sharon sighed. "Oh, why did we have to leave so soon? An hour from now I'll be wondering if it all happened."

"Borg's a workman," Seay said curtly.

It irritated Sharon the moment he said it. "Of course, but don't workmen stay up late? Who packs the saloons till dawn?"

"Not Borg's kind," Seay said firmly. "Right now, Borg is sitting over books. And what he gets out of those books will make him an engineer some day. He's come as far as muscle can bring him—for a mucker to an expert driller. It's not enough."

"Oh, I didn't know," Sharon murmured.

They were silent then, but Sharon was happy and disturbed and a little bit sad too.

Suddenly Seay said, "No, that wasn't the reason I wanted to leave either."

Sharon looked up at him, but in the dark his face was only a dark high blur.

"Then what was it?" she asked.

Seay made an inarticulate gesture with the arm Sharon had her hand on, and then he laughed shortly. "Have you ever seen a kid stand in front of a show-case full of candy and punish himself by looking at it? The sensible kid walks away, and I'm old enough to be sensible."

After a pause, Sharon said slowly, "Punish himself. I've never thought of it that way."

"Yes, punish himself." He, too, was quiet a moment. "Borg has everything a man wants to make his life. He and Kristin have made it for themselves. They know where they're going and they'll get there, and when he lies down to die he'll be ready to laugh like hell."

Sharon was astonished at the quiet passion in his voice. "Laugh? But why?"

"He's beat the game," Seay said simply. "Even if a man isn't born to suffer like they tell us, he soon picks up the ability. He tries to beat it all his life, and if he's lucky, he can. Borg can. He already has."

"Then Borg and his life are the candy in the show-case and you're the boy—the boy who walks away."

"That's right," Seay said shortly.

Sharon did not speak for a moment, and then she laughed huskily, softly. "How strange you are," she murmured, "how hard—even on yourself."

"The man who doesn't get hurt is the man who won't let himself be," Seay countered.

"You envy Borg then?"

Seay considered this a moment before he answered. "Yes. That's what I want, what he's got. Not the same wife or the same children, or the same possessions, maybe, but what he's got; that's my life. It's got balance and—and hard-headedness."

"Why is it so different?" Sharon asked quietly.

"It isn't soft or easy or safe," Seay answered, just as quietly. "It doesn't ask for any help or take any, but it always gives it. What's wrong with envying that?"

"Nothing," Sharon murmured. "It's—it's just strange to, that's all."

"To you, maybe," Seay said carefully.

Sharon felt the reproof in his words, and tiny anger flared up within her. "To me. Am I so different, then?"

"From Borg, from me, from Kristin, yes."

Sharon stopped, and Seay swung around to face her.

"How am I different, then?" Sharon demanded.

"You've hunted for the soft all your life, haven't you?" Seay asked quietly. "It's nothing to be ashamed about. Most people do. You have. It's money and ease and comfort. You look for it always, even in your men."

"I do not!" Sharon protested passionately.

Seay's face fell into its usual reserve. "All right then, you don't."

"What right have you to judge me for something I can't help?" Sharon went on. "How do you know I'm satisfied with what I have or the way I live? How do you?"

"Maybe I don't," Seay admitted.

"No, you don't," Sharon said more quietly. "The only times I get out of the stupid squirrel cage are times like these," she added.

Seay swung around and they walked on. Sharon felt that if she could pour out all her discontent to him he would understand, but how was she to hide the fact that it was he, Phil Seay, who had bred this discontent in her? How could she dodge it? And if he ever guessed it, she would die of shame. She held her head proudly and did not speak of it again.

When he left her at the door of the suite, Sharon saw he was puzzled, and felt the questions that lay unanswered behind the reserve in his eyes. His good-bye was almost formal, and then he smiled oddly and said, "Maybe I've got to pick up my blocks and arrange them all over again—about you."

Sharon nodded gravely. "If it matters, yes."

He was about to ask a question, but his mouth closed and he nodded and left her.

Chapter XVI

He listened to Craig, thinking that this was something he did not like, and he took a firmer grasp on his attention, following Craig's words and his pencil as he pointed occasionally to the unfolded plans laid on the desk. Sills, lintels, yardage and concrete mix, form lumber, apprentice masons, the tensile strength of pine compared to oak, and the probable inaccuracy of trying to calculate the shrinkage of half-seasoned timbers. He was glad when Tober stepped in the door, waiting. Craig, irritated now, knowing Tober would take Seay off with him, finally gave up and looked over at Tober.

"Take a look outside," Tober said.

Seay went out with him. The ditch which cut down from the tunnel mouth and continued past the new mill foundations to the dry river-bed was running water, more water than usual.

"When did that start?" Seay asked.

"I dunno. I just noticed it. They've had to quit work on the trench."

Seay glanced up at the tunnel mouth. "Maybe they hit a water pocket at the Dry Sierras."

"Maybe," Reed said.

"Call me if it doesn't slack off," Seay said. "Lay off the crew for the afternoon." He returned to his business with Craig. Half an hour later, Tober reported that, far from slacking off, the volume of water was increasing. Seay ordered a horse saddled, and when it was brought up, he left Craig and headed out of camp for the pass.

At the Dry Sierras Consolidated he left his horse at the tie-rail of the office and tramped up the slope to the shaft-house. Its doors were opened wide and he could hear the labouring of the hoist engine as the cages of ore were raised and dumped. It was a hum of activity inside. Of a workman at the door, he asked for Sales, the superintendent, and the man led him around the building. In its shade Sales was squatted, drawing a crude map on the ground for five workmen.

Seay waited until he was finished, and then Sales, a middle-aged man with sparse grey hair and deeply sunburned face, came over to him. They exchanged small talk a few minutes, and then Seay asked, "Hit a water pocket to-day?"

Sales shook his head. "Nobody said anything to me about it. Why?"

"Where's all the extra water coming from?"

Sales said, "Oh," and gestured across the slope to a huge building perhaps a half-mile off. It was where the shaft for four mines—the Southern Union, Bismarck, Petersburg and Pacific Shares—went down into the Pintwaters. It was a huge affair, housing the main pump. The single shaft was used by all four mines, and was on the common corner of all four claims. "Pump shaft broke," he said laconically. "The water backed up to Gallery H level, and now it's coming through to us. Do you mind?"

Seay shook his head. "I've had to lay off a crew. It's quite a head of water. They got a crew on repairs now?"

"They came over to me and said they were putting one on. That was early this morning."

Seay chatted a moment longer and then left. In Tronah he picked up some light freight at the office and rode back to the tunnel.

But by mid-afternoon the water had nearly doubled its flow out of the mouth of the tunnel, and Tober reported that it had been increasing hourly. Still, Seay worked through the afternoon, giving it little attention. He did not intend to raise any objection, for, obviously, the four mines had run into a little hard luck with their pumps. A little tolerance on his part would help correct the trouble. But when at four o'clock the flow was still increasing in volume, he saddled a horse and rode across to the Big Four, which was the more usable name for the four mines.

He hunted out Pedro Sais, the works superintendent, who was working on the pump. Sais was a big, good-looking Mexican employed by all four mines to oversee all the work above ground, and his honesty, of course, had never been in doubt. It was his work to keep track of which ore raised in the common shaft belonged to which outfit, besides superintending the machinery.

He walked out to Seay, wiping his hands with cotton waste.

"What's the trouble, Pedro?" Seay asked him.

"She's busted casting," Pedro said grimly. "Plenty busted. *Por dios,* I start her and the shaft, she's bust too."

"Casting," Seay murmured, watching Sais carefully. "That means freighting from San Francisco, doesn't it?"

"*Si, señor.* It is true."

"Six days, then, before you can use it again?"

"Seven, *señor,* is safer."

Seay left then. Obviously Sais was not the man to argue with. It was Hugh Mathias who was allowing water from the Big Four to be diverted to his shaft. But riding down the freight road that turned off to the Dry Sierras, something warned Seay to play cautious. At Tronah he stabled his horse and went straight to the Union House. Bonal was in his office, and Seay took a chair and told him what had happened. Bonal listened to it, frowning, and when he had heard Seay out, he said, "You're worried, Phil. Why?"

"I haven't said I was."

"I know, but you look it. What does it mean, except that the Big Four expects the Dry Sierras to be a good neighbour and Hugh expects to be one in turn?"

"Did Mathias say that?"

"I don't think he knows about it," Bonal said. "He's up in the mountains hunting with a couple of Dry Sierras directors. I'll tell him to-morrow when he gets back." He shrugged. "What harm does it do?"

"None—except that trench crew can't work till it slacks off."

"All right. I'll talk with Hugh to-morrow."

It was left that way. Seay went back to the tunnel and spent an uneasy evening playing poker with Tober and Craig and Lueter.

In the morning the tunnel was running more water than ever. It was a torrent now, waist deep to a man, and pouring out of the tunnel trench in a great cascade that more than filled the mill-run. As Seay regarded it, his eyes narrowed thoughtfully. There was more than just the overflow from the Big Four coming out. Mentally he calculated. The trench they were digging to carry the water under the tracks had been designed to accommodate all the water from most of the mines in this field. And this flow now was more than filling the short stretch of trench already dug.

He saddled a horse. It was early, and the camp was still in shadow. His destination, of course, was Bonal, but he planned to make a detour before going to Tronah, and he turned off and rode up the mountain to the Big Four shaft.

Round the corner of the office, he headed up to the shaft-house. As he rode, he saw men gathering in its door, and he smiled thinly.

Reaching them, he pulled up his horse but did not dismount. Pedro Sais, smiling affably, stood in the door. He was holding a wrench now, and his crew around him were alert, their faces shaped for trouble. They had been expecting him, Seay knew instantly.

"Not fixed yet, Pedro?" Seay asked easily.

"Not yet, *señor,*" Pedro answered.

"Did all the other pumps in all the other shafts break too, Pedro?" Seay drawled.

"I don't understand, *señor,*" Pedro replied easily.

"You liar," Seay said quietly, his voice steel under velvet. "We're getting water from every mine on this field. It's coming into your shaft and running out into the Dry Sierras."

Sais shrugged, still politely. "That is your business, *señor,*" he answered affably. "If they want to divert their water to us, it does not matter. Our shaft is filling anyway."

Seay nodded curtly and swung his horse around. He began to understand it now, understand what Vannie had been trying to tell him. He cursed himself for his blindness. But swiftly his thoughts turned to the crux of the trouble. It was the Dry Sierras. Bonal would handle that.

At the hotel Bonal was breakfasting with Sharon. The table had been laid in Bonal's office. At sight of Seay, Bonal motioned him to a chair, saying, "Up early, Phil."

Seay nodded to Sharon and did not answer. He did not sit down either.

"Well, Bonal," he drawled calmly, "your friends have hatched an egg that'll take a lot of breaking."

Bonal knew what Seay was thinking when he used that voice. He looked up swiftly. "What?"

"All the water in the Tronah field—with the exception of

Vannie Shore's Golgotha—is being dumped into your tunnel."

Bonal said slowly, "How?"

"Through the Dry Sierras shaft. The broken pump story of the Big Four was a lie. All they wanted was time to get the water from the other mines flowing into their shaft and then into the Dry Sierras."

"Ah," Bonal said softly. "Did they do it?"

"The tunnel is carrying all the water in the Tronah field right now."

Bonal called sharply, "Sarita!" When the maid appeared, Bonal said, "Go bring Hugh Mathias up here. He'll be in the dining-room."

Sharon wanted to say something, but she saw it was not the time. A tension was mounting in her as she cleared the table of breakfast things. When she finished, she returned to the room, and Bonal looked up at her.

"You leave us alone a while, Sharon," he said gruffly.

"I don't intend to," Sharon answered quietly, firmly. "I have a right to hear this."

Bonal stared at her and then turned away. A few minutes later Hugh appeared. He was fresh shaven, dressed in a neat dark suit, and he smiled at Sharon as he greeted her. Seay, leaning against the wall, arms folded across his chest, returned Hugh's greeting with a nod. Bonal did not return it at all.

Bonal said shortly, "Hugh, has anyone told you that all the mines in this Tronah field are draining their water through your gallery into out tunnel?"

Hugh nodded, his face gradually losing its affability. "Sales said the Big Four were draining through our gallery. Their pump broke."

"That was yesterday. To-day every pump in the Tronah field has stopped. All their water is coming through the Big Four shaft to us."

"What do you want me to do?" Hugh asked slowly.

"Stop it! Block up the gallery!"

Hugh said carefully, "I'm sorry but I'm powerless to make a move without consulting the directors."

Bonal's eyes narrowed. "Directors, huh? Weren't you hunting with a couple of them yesterday?"

"Maybe this is why he was," Seay drawled gently.

Bonal ignored this but Hugh did not. His wicked glance touched Seay and returned to Bonal.

"Are they here in the hotel?" Bonal demanded, and when Hugh said they were, he added curtly, "Get them!"

Seay packed his pipe while Hugh was gone. Bonal lighted one of his black cigars and puffed furiously on it. He was behind his desk, staring intently at its top, as if he were regarding something upon it. Sharon sat motionless in a corner and watched these two men. They were both trying not to look at her, she knew, and she felt a hot shame. But stubbornly, doggedly, she told herself she was going to hear this out.

Hugh came in with Freehold, the lawyer Bonal had met, and a heavier, squatter man named Barton McCauley. As soon as the introductions were made, Bonal did not bother to ask them to be seated.

His voice was hard, driving, belligerent as he spoke. He told them the bare facts of the happenings, and concluded with, "Mathias tells me he can't act without your consent. Is that right?"

Freehold nodded. He was obviously enjoying his after-breakfast cigar.

"Then I want you to give it," Bonal said abruptly. "This is a conspiracy to evade a legal obligation."

"In other words, you think it's illegal, Mr. Bonal?" Freehold asked.

"I do."

Freehold smiled meagrely. "Its legality allows no doubt, Bonal. I made sure of that before I planned it, Mathias"—he gestured to Hugh with his cigar—"of course, being completely in the dark. The act is entirely legal. Do you remember the gist of the contract signed between Mathias and yourself?"

"Certainly," Bonal snapped. "I was to put in a tunnel of the specified height and width which would drain all water from the Dry Sierras Consolidated shaft at a depth of——"

"That's far enough," Freehold said. He turned and smiled at McCauley. "All water, I think you said, Bonal. I can't recall the contract specifying that water from other mines couldn't be diverted to our shafts."

Bonal started to speak and then checked himself, the light dawning in his eye. "So that's it, eh?" he said grimly.

Freehold nodded. "That's it. You're legally bound to drain all water from the Dry Sierras Consolidated shaft at the depth mentioned. In return, the Dry Sierras pays you the specified amount per ton *of all ore drained by your tunnel that is taken from within our boundaries*." He paused and raised his cigar slowly to his mouth. "It's in black and white, Bonal, signed and sealed, and every court in the country will uphold it."

Bonal's teeth clamped down on his cigar until the end of it

sagged. Slowly he withdrew it from his mouth, bitten almost in two, and held it in his hand. Seay saw the veins in his temples standing out.

"Why, you fools," Bonal said in a low, angry voice, "I'll blow that tunnel in before I'll stand for that!"

McCauley spoke up then in a throaty growl. "Don't forget your other obligation, Bonal," he said. "The rest of your contract calls for your hauling our ore and milling it for a specified amount." He shrugged his heavy shoulders. "If you can drain our shafts and mill our ore at the price agreed upon and signed for, and without the help of the tunnel, then you're at liberty to cave-in every foot of it. Otherwise, I wouldn't advise it."

Bonal looked from McCauley to Freehold. "I see. I'm tied legally. I get paid for draining one mine, when I drain every mine in this field. I'll go bankrupt, and be forced to sell. Then you'll buy. Is that it, gentlemen?"

"Roughly," Freehold nodded. He could not help giving a twist to the knife. "That's so simple, even you can understand it, Bonal."

Bonal did not wince outwardly. He asked in a calm voice, "This is Janeece's scheme, of course."

"He is one of our associates," Freehold said. He dropped his cigar in an ash-tray and said, "Is that all, Bonal? We understand each other?"

"Perfectly," Bonal said.

"Then you can always get in touch with us through Janeece. I'm certain he'll give you a reasonably fair figure for the tunnel, and for the building site of your mill. Good-day, sir."

They turned to the door. Hugh took a step to join them, when Bonal said, "You stay, Hugh."

When McCauley and Freehold were gone, Bonal said to Hugh, "Sit down."

Hugh did. Bonal went over to confront him. "Are you still manager of the Dry Sierras Consolidated?"

"In name, I suppose."

"The men take your orders?"

Hugh nodded.

"All right," Bonal said. "Give them orders to stop this diversion of water. If these two blackguards oust you from the management for doing it, that'll be all right. In two months I'll have the biggest milling company in the Tronah field in operation. You'll be its manager and you'll draw the same salary you're drawing now. Furthermore, you'll have a juicy cut of the stock. All I'm asking in return is that you order them to effective stop this diversion of water and make it stick! Can you?"

Tiny beads of sweat showed on Hugh's forehead. He looked at Sharon, who watched him, her eyes steady and unblinking and proud.

Hugh said quietly, "What good would that do?"

"I want time," Bonal said harshly. "I'll think of something! I'll block the tunnel so it can't be used."

"But you can't!" Hugh said.

Bonal stared at him, his face changing a little. "I made you a proposition. Will you take it?" he asked coldly.

Hugh looked at Sharon one agonising instant, pleading and fear in his eyes. But Sharon's still face was impassive, waiting. Slowly, then, Hugh rose and when he was erect he shook his head. "I can't, Bonal. I'd like to. But if I do, I ruin a career I've set my heart on. Besides, I haven't the authority. They'd——"

Bonal cursed him, and swung on his heel and walked to the desk. Hugh stood for a brief moment, seeking help in Sharon's face, and when he did not find it, when he found only contempt in those cool eyes, he wheeled and left the room.

Bonal walked over to Sharon and said quietly, "I don't think this'll break your heart, do you, honey?"

Sharon shook her head.

"Then forget it," Bonal said, touching her hand. "I made the same mistake about Hugh that you did. Forget it."

Sharon rose and left the room. Seay did not look at her, and she did not look at him. As she approached the door to the parlour she ran a little, as if the thought of being here longer was unbearable.

Bonal sank down in his chair and lighted a fresh cigar. Seay walked over to the chair opposite the desk and sat on its arm, facing Bonal.

"Have they got me, Phil?" Bonal asked finally.

Seay did not answer at all. Presently he rose and walked to the window and stood looking down at the street, his face frowning. Finally he asked, "Have you got the Dry Sierras contract here?"

"No. It's at the tunnel office," Bonal said wearily.

"Maybe," Seay said slowly. "Maybe they can't." He half turned to face Bonal. "Isn't there a clause in that contract that says the tunnel must be finished? McCauley and Freehold might be right as to the legality of it, but isn't all that preceded by the clause, 'Upon completion of said tunnel, such and such must be done'?"

"Of course," Bonal said idly.

"But the tunnel isn't done," Seay pointed out slowly. "We've still got that drain trench to complete."

"What of it?"

"Then they can't lawfully divert their water to you until you're ready for it."

"What good would that do?" Bonal asked sharply, some of the fight back in his voice.

"Then make them hold this water back until you're finished. And when you've got their water shut off, build a bulkhead in the tunnel that will stop the flow of water. Then you can take three years to complete the drain trench, if you want to take it. Before that, hey'll have struck *borrasca* and will be ready to talk business."

"But the water's there," Bonal said grimly. "Janeece will see that it stays there."

Seay said, "Yes," slowly, looking at Bonal.

Bonal was looking at him too. "Bulkhead," he murmured. "Can you put a bulkhead in the tunnel? With this head of water running?"

"It's risky," Seay said mildly.

"But can you do it?"

Seay walked over to Bonal's desk and stood before it. "Yes, I can do it," he said gently, his voice carrying an edge to it. "I can risk the necks of men, maybe drown some. Maybe I can do a good job of it. I don't know. The point is, Bonal, that water doesn't belong there. It's got no right there. It's a matter of principle."

"But what can I do?" Bonal said, his voice almost angry now.

"I know what I'd do," Seay countered. "I'd shut that water off."

"How?"

"You want me to show you?" Seay asked quietly.

"I want you to tell me."

"I won't tell you," Seay said stubbornly, almost jeering. "I asked if you wanted me to show you?"

The two men looked at each other. Bonal was trying to see, to feel what was behind Seay's attitude, and he could not. And he had a sense of foreboding about it. But Bonal was not a quitter. "Yes, show me, then," he said quietly.

Seay laughed softly, turned and went out.

Chapter XVII

Tober sucked on a cold pipe and occasionally parted the brush from before him and looked down through it. From where he was squatted, he could get a clear view of the Dry Sierras shaft-house. The last workman had filed out the doorway, dinner bucket over shoulder, and turned to say something to the night watchman and stoker, then had gone on.

Tober's glance raised to a vent-pipe in the roof where a plume of steam reached up and vanished. He turned to Seay then and said, "Just a little longer."

"No guards?"

"Not unless they're inside."

They waited a few minutes more and then left the screening brush. Seay was carrying a coil of rope, two drills, and a fat package was pressed under his arm.

At the shaft-house they tried the door, and it swung open on to the gloom of the interior. It was a huge building, some three storeys high. A third of the way down it, huge beams laced across the roof, and it was from these that the tackle for the car and skip hoists swung. The shaft-head itself was collared off, and the iron shaft car stood empty at floor level, a lantern still burning swung from its roof. Beyond, a track ran the length of the building, past huge piles of ore and out an open door in the rear to the dump-heap. Here was where the ore was sorted and graded and sacked previous to freighting. To the right, the hoist engines and pumps were looming blackly. The pump, its great rocker-arms idle now, was a thing of the past since the tunnel completion.

Tober turned immediately to his right and headed for the doorway that let on to the furnace-room. Inside it, propped against its jamb, a heavy-muscled man in a cotton singlet sat in a chair, his lunch-bucket beside him, a sandwich in his fist.

At the sound of their approach, he turned to confront the gun held in Tober's hand, and his jaw slacked open.

"Get up and stoke the fires, fella," Reed said quietly, nodding towards the huge furnaces. "We need steam."

It was a moment before the man understood. Then he closed his mouth and swallowed, and made a vague gesture with his sandwich. "We—we've quit work here, mister."

"Not yet," Tober said. "You're goin' to keep steam up for

the hoist engine. I'll sit here and watch you. But first"—his head nodded to Seay behind him—"you'll put the cage down to Gallery G for him."

The man stood speechless as Seay took one of the candle lanterns from the wall rack holding dozens of them and lighted it. He disappeared in the gloom of the shed, to return a few moments later with a light sledge which, together with the rest of his equipment, he put on the floor of the cage.

"How many shells you got?" Tober asked.

"Enough," was Seay's grim answer. Rammed in his belt was his cedar-handled Colt revolver. He closed the safety gate of the car and stood there waiting while Tober prodded the stoker over to the hoist engine. There was a slow grinding of gears and the cage started to sink. Seay's last sight of Tober was memorable. Gun in one hand, he was lighting his pipe with the other. And then the car started its fall.

Now the walls slid by so swiftly that they were a blur. Gallery after gallery was passed, a yawning pitch-black hole that appeared and disappeared swiftly as down, down the car went, the cables above it whispering tautly. It was an interminable ride. The car clanked against the cage's guide irons, lurched a little, but never slowed down. All of the earth seemed to have folded about him, leaving only this sliding panel of rock, now shiny with water, whipping by him.

Then the car slowed, pressing the floor up against his boot-soles. Now it settled gently and came to a full stop, facing and level with the black pit of a gallery. Seay swung open the safety gate and unloaded his gear. Then he stood on the edge of the gallery listening. Below him, he could not tell how far, he heard the swift hissing of pouring water. Far, far below, it thundered into the choked tunnel-head.

Taking his lantern, he set out down the gallery, his eyes roving its partially-timbered sides. His pace was slow, as if he were looking for something. At each cross-drift, or dead-end tunnel that forked off from the gallery proper, he turned in, and, lantern held high, paced its length. He was looking for a winze, or a shaft sunk from this level that would let him down to the next gallery. For down there, one gallery lower, was H gallery, where this river of turgid water was emptying into the shaft and the tunnel.

Each time he came upon the dead end of the cross-drift, he would patiently turn back to the gallery and try the next drift. It was laborious, slow work, maybe fruitless. He did not know.

At a station, or a cut back in the gallery where the mines'

gear was stored, he turned in, and this time walked straight to its far corner. There was a square hold there in its floor, the ends of a ladder poking out. Swinging on to the ladder, he disappeared for a moment, then reappeared and walked back the several hundred yards to the gallery mouth. The car was still there, its lantern glowing in this hot air. This time he picked up all his gear and brought it back to the winze mouth.

First, then, he tied the rope about his waist and slung the coil over his shoulder. The sledge handle he rammed through his belt, so that his arms would be free for the lantern and the two long drills nestled in the crook of his arm.

Swinging on to the top rungs of the ladder, he lowered himself into the winze. As he climbed down, far, far down, the full sound of running water came more and more distinctly to his ears. When finally he had passed the roof of the H gallery he swung his lantern out, looking below him. This was also a station, and the great lake of water coiled in slow, black eddies below him. Holding the lantern higher, he squinted out, and saw in the gallery proper the smooth surface of the millrace that was flowing down its length.

Satisfied, he regarded the ladder. It was held to the rock of the wall by iron cleats, and its timbers were substantial. He tied the end of his rope to the timber, then, holding the lantern higher, lowered himself into the water. It came up above his waist, and was warm, almost comfortable. Playing out the rope, he waded across the eddy and was soon approaching the gallery. He could feel the tug of the water around his legs now.

Steadying himself, he moved on again, this time out into the stream. Its current almost picked up his feet, but he leaned against the rope, holding the lantern and the two drills high. Then he was in the full current, and it whipped him back against the wall, tugging at his legs with its swift, ponderous strength. Foot by foot, he let out the rope, going down the gallery. He was looking at the walls, and now he stopped.

For a moment he stood motionless, the water rushing up almost to his chest. Then, holding the lantern bale in his teeth, he reached in shirt pocket and drew out a spike and rammed it head-high in a crack of the rock wall and tested it. It was solid. This was for the lantern, which he slung there. Now he worked down a few feet and, satisfied, took a full minute to work the long drill down inside his belt. Now his hands were free. Pulling the sledge out of his belt and taking one of the drills, he spread his feet, braced himself against the rope, and started to work. Slowly, slowly, the drills were sledged into the rock. When he sunk the length of the short drill, he pulled out the long drill and sunk it deeper. And after each hole was drilled he moved on down-stream and drilled another. His work had a sustained, dogged patience that was backed by a savage will. Not once did he take time to rest, his sledging as regular as the ticking of a watch. It was hours before he had all the holes drilled, and then throwing the sledge and the short drill into the stream, he pulled himself upstream to the station and climbed the ladder. His lantern was back there in the gallery, but he did not need it. He sat a moment at the head of the ladder, resting, his head hung in weariness, his breathing deep and fast. Presently he fumbled in the dark for the rest of his gear, and then lowered himself again. This time, once in the water, with no lantern to carry, the going was easy. The fat package was held high out of the water, and he played himself down the rope swiftly. He went to the farthest hole first, and worked up.

In each hole he placed his dynamite, and rammed it back gently with the drill, careful not to be rough with the fuse-caps and the lenth of fuse. At each hole he did the same; and, finished, he threw his drill into the stream and let himself down to the farthermost hole again. This time he held the candle of the lantern in his hand.

Swiftly, then, as swiftly as this water would let him move, he lighted the fuses, making sure first they were not wet, and arranging them so they would not trail into the water. He moved up, lighting each one.

When the last was lighted he looked down the gloom of the gallery, the oily race of the water reflecting the many burning fuses.

Then he put the candle in the lantern and made his way to the winze, his face haggard with weariness. Once up the ladder, clothes dripping, he strapped on his gun and went into the gallery, turning towards the shaft.

He stopped. The car was not there.

For one brief instant he stood high and motionless, his face alert, strained. It was not the dynamite gathering to explode below that he was afraid of. It was the fact that Tober had told him the car would remain there. And now it was gone.

He felt a slow, gathering expectancy flood through him. Then he turned and went down the gallery, his lantern swinging at his knees. He was looking back over his shoulder when the explosion came. It was rumbling, its echo slapping out into the main shaft and up it and into this gallery, so that it was muffled, but the earth rocked beneath him and rock clattered down from the roof and the walls under the slow heaving.

He stood motionless a moment, his eyes still on the gallery end. Why not go back and down the winze to see if the shots had formed the dam he knew they would? But caution told him to go on, to lose himself some way in this labyrinth of galleries before he was discovered.

Slowly, then, he started back to the winze. He had gone only a few steps when he saw the car swing down into the shaft. His motion in extinguishing the lantern was as swift as sight, but he knew he was too late, and he cursed. He stood there for one moment, watching the men boil out of the cage, shouting. A shot ripped and hammered echoes through the gallery, and on its heels a man shouted, "Straight down! I saw his light! He's there!"

It was the voice of Chris Feldhake. Seasy turned into a drift, and put his lantern down and drew his gun. There were three lanterns among these ten men, and they bobbed furiously, casting jerking shadows against the gallery walls.

Seay shot into the floor, and abruptly the men stopped running. One by one their lights went out. Seay lighted his own then, and set it in the drift mouth. He could hear the soft footfalls of the approaching ten.

Suddenly he called out in a loud voice, "No closer, boys. I've still got dynamite enough to take care of you."

The echo of his voice had already died when Ferd Yates's voice called, "Seay!"

"Yes."

"Come out of there! You're caught clean!"

Seay laughed softly. "Try again, Ferd."

There was another long silence. Somebody tried to shoot the lantern out, and the slug nicked the corner of the wall and sang down the gallery. But the lantern was protected by the corner.

"Seay, I say!" Ferd called again. "We've got you! I'll send the boys up the next gallery and they'll pass you and come down, and you'll be trapped. Throw out that gun and dynamite!"

"To Feldhake?" Seay answered. "No, I'll take my killin' from the front, and with a gun in my hand."

"What do you want then?" Yates called.

"Send that mob of killers up on top, Yates, before I blow us all up!" Seay answered.

A long pause, and a murmur of voices.

"You surrender if I do?" Yates asked.

"To you, yes. To you alone. To the rest, no, and to hell with you!"

"You can't beat this job, Seay!" Ferd called angrily. "We'll get you if we have to cave the whole gallery on top you!"

"Send Feldhake up on top," Seay countered. "If you don't like that talk, let's fight."

There was an angry murmur of voices down the gallery. "By God, we'll smoke you out," someone called angrily, and Seay did not answer. Clearly he calculated his chances of escaping. There weren't any. These men knew these drifts and galleries, and they could corner him and soon force his bluff as to the dynamite. All that he had between himself and capture was a belt of shells. But to walk out there and give himself up to Feldhake and Yates was to assure himself of a shot in the back. No witnesses that wouldn't lie afterwards, no justice—only death. He would not do it.

He struck a match. They could see that flare, and maybe guess what it meant. They did. There was a swift pounding of feet, and he let the match die, laughing softly.

This time Yates's voice came from farther down the gallery. "Seay, you got a chance if you give up. You ain't got a sign of a one if you stay!"

"Who's with you?" Seay asked.

Yates named them over. One was Sales, the Dry Sierras super, another Tim Prince, an honest gambler in Tronah. As for the rest, they were saloon riffraff, corralled by Feldhake. Prince, Sales and Yates were honest men in their way, certainly not murderers.

Leave Sales and Prince here, and send the rest back to town, Yates," Seay said finally. "I'll surrender to you then. But I'll keep my gun."

This led to a hot argument, the details of which he could not distinguish. Finally Yates called, "All right. They're goin'."

"Wait, Ferd," Seay said levelly. "I haven't finished. Get Bonal down here. When I can hear him, I'll come out. I'll give myself up to you, then."

This started another furious argument. Somebody shot down the gallery, trying for the lamp again. A cold fury boiled up in Seay and he sent back a shot in reply. He heard a man curse him in low, vicious tones, and then the arugment started again.

It was a full ten minutes before Yates called, "All right. I've sent 'em up. Bonal will be down when we find him."

" Good," Seay said. He heard the men tramp down to the car, and heard it start its ascent. His hearing strained wire-taut now, he listened for the others. There was a murmuring down the way. It could be a trap, he knew. Feldhake could go up one gallery and come down on his other side, trying to surprise him. What had happened to Tober? Reed would fight. Now the silence was absolute, a warning, drawn-out silence that rang in his ears with every movement of his blood.

Slowly he backed into the drift, beyond the light of the lantern, and waited. His eyes searched out that flat expanse of gallery wall for any tell-tale movement. There was none. And time did not pass, stood still, and he waited, the silence riding him with its threat.

It seemed hours until he heard the car return and the lone footsteps of a man approach. There was some low talk, and then Bonal said, " Phil!"

Seay's breath soughed out in a great gust and he relaxed. He rammed the gun in his belt, and picked up the lantern and walked up to Bonal, Yates, Prince and Sales.

Bonal's face held a mixture of anger and relief.

Seay stopped in front of him. " You said to show you," he said quietly. " I did. That water's shut off. Get Borg to slap a bulkhead in the tunnel now."

Bonal's jaw slacked open a little. He said, " You—this was what you meant?"

Seay said harshly, " Bonal, maybe I'm not like you. But a man can ride me just so long. Janeece, Feldhake, Mathias rode me just long enough."

Yates said in vicious gloating, " Not *quite* enough, Seay. Not after this."

Neither Bonal nor Seay paid him any attention. Bonal said quietly, " Tober's up there. Dead. Shot in the back."

Seay stared at him one brief moment, and then his wicked glance swung full on Yates.

Yates nosed up his gun and backed off. " He fought, you fool!" Yates cried. " Feldhake shot him! It was the only way he could get down!"

" Ah," Seay said quietly. He stood motionless, his fists clenched so that the knuckles showed a blue white, and then he looked away from Yates.

" All right, let's go," he said in a voice that was quiet, dead, beaten.

Chapter XVIII

Bonal demanded the preliminary hearing in the morning, and got it. It was a half-hearted hearing, motivated by a revenge that could not be adequate, for Borg and his crew had worked the night through to make the bulkhead. It was finished, blocking every drop of water from entering the Bonal Tunnel. Hugh Mathias and the men back of him had not even pulled out a crew to clear the gallery after the explosion. The water had been dammed by the shot and it would take days for it to back up through all the dozen mines to flood a higher gallery. The very act of Seay's violence with its savage daring had beaten them. Bonal had only to wait now for *borrasca* to touch them.

The questions at the hearing were perfunctory. Seay, a trace of a black beard stubble on his face, admitted to everything, and a high bail was set, which Bonal paid promptly, and they were dismissed. The gun which was returned to him Seay stuck in his belt. His face was haggard, overlaid with a weariness that was not relaxed.

Bonal took him into a saloon and they ordered drinks and took seats, but when their drinks came, Bonal found he had nothing to say. His fight was won, clinched by an act of violence that awed him. And remaining was only the victory, and Tober's death, one cancelling the other. He felt old and weary and sad, and he pitied the man across from him. For the cold grief in Seay's eyes was a thing that Bonal did not like to watch.

"You better sleep," Bonal said gently.

"Afterwards."

Bonal was about to ask, "After what?" and then it came to him that he might have understood before this. He paid for the score and rose, and said, "I can't help, can I?"

When Seay shook his head, Bonal left. Seay went out later and tramped into a store and purchased a box of shells. He stood by the counter, a high, straight figure, wearing the same clothes of last night, which had dried in folds and sharp wrinkles. His shirt, torn at the back, was foul with all the dirt of the water. He took five shells from the box he had purchased, loaded his gun, let the hammer fall on the empty chamber, and then rammed the gun in the waistband of his trousers.

"You keep the rest for me," he told the clerk, leaving the rest of the cartridges.

And now he started that old hunt which was so familiar to him in the past, and which had been interrupted once before. Feldhake was not at the Melodian.

Swinging out its door, he almost bumped into Vannie Shore, who was on the way to her buggy at the hitch-rail. She put out a hand and Seay stopped, and Vannie said softly, "I heard about it, Phil. It's frand and it's sad, and no fun winning."

Seay nodded mutely. Vannie said, "You've got to do it, haven't you, Phil?"

Again he nodded. "Then, bless you, finish it," Vannie told him and left him.

Seay was later to remember that, although it slipped from his mind now, like something trivial and almost unheard. It was as if there were no room in his mind for anything but the quiet indictments which he had arranged in an orderly and understandable fashion. First there was the poker game, and then Hardiston, and then Jimmy Hamp's murder, and then the cave-in, and now Tober. Tough, lovable Reed Tober, who had died with a slug in his back. A clean way to die, yes, but the wrong way, and thinking of it, the cool, merciless fury of memory swept over him.

Feldhake was not at the Union House bar. Shouldering out its door, he saw Charles and Sharon Bonal on their way from the dining-room through the lobby. Sharon was wearing a blue dress that crowned all her fragile loveliness, and she stopped, and paid no attention to Bonal's murmured words for her to come on. She was in front of Seay, and he paused now and took off his hat. His hair was untidy and matted, and she looked first at his haunted face and then at his hair, and small tears glistened in the corners of her eyes.

"I hope," Sharon said in a small voice. "I hope——" She did not go on. She laid her hand momentarily on Seay's arm, and then bowed her head and went on.

He was to remember this afterwards, too, and differently. Patience was easy now. At the Full Mile, he could tell by the way the bartender told him Feldhake wasn't here that they knew, that the word was getting around. Soon now, he thought.

At the head of the street he crossed and came down the other side, and he already had his shoulder against the bat-wing doors of the Miners' Rest, when his glance swung down the street and he stopped.

A man was coming up the walk, and the way was cleared of people between them now. He swung deliberately on his heel.

It was the shambling gait of the man that made Seay smile faintly, and he walked past the saloon and a saddle shop towards him. Under the wood awnings here it was almost cool. Or was it that?

He stopped in front of the saddle shop. Beyond it, by a tiny weed-grown wedge of land that was stacked with empty beer barrels, Feldhake stopped too. His thick legs were a little spread, and both thumbs were looped in his belt.

Seay's wicked gaze touched his face and then dropped down to his chest, and noted the row of cigars in his breast pocket, and noted, too, that Feldhake's hands had left his belts and were gripped about the butts of the two guns slung low at his hips.

Seay felt the grip of his own revolver warm and smooth against his palm, and as he raised it he saw Feldhake shoot from one gun and then from the other, savagely, handling them like clubs with a short chopping stroke.

Carefully, then, he swung up his own gun, his breath stilled, and when his sight lined with the five cigars in the shirt pocket, he fired. Once.

He watched, then, gun slack at his side, while Feldhake shot again into the board-walk almost at his feet, and then fell on his knees and then on his face.

Walking up to him, Seay touched him once with the toe of his boot. The flesh under his boot was soft and relaxed, and then he looked up at the people crowding around him.

Yates was there now. Men were talking to Yates, pointing to Feldhake and then to Seay. Seay waited and nothing happened, and he turned away, breaking through the crowd. It was seconds later that he realised he was still holding the gun in his hand. He threw it on to the steps of a store, and saw it fall at a woman's feet, brushing her skirt as it came to rest. And he looked up and saw that the woman was Vannie, who had been watching him.

He did not seem to know her, and she turned slowly and disappeared in the store. Swinging under the hitch-rack, he threaded his way through the wagons blocking the way to the Union House.

Tramping up the stairs, a bitter weariness dragged at him and smothered his movements to slowness.

He opened the door to Bonal's office and stood there, hand on knob. Sharon, at the window, was looking at him, her face still, contained, utterly lovely. Bonal stood before his desk.

Seay said, "I'll be drifting, Bonal," but he watched Sharon, saw the life come into her face.

"You didn't go to her," Sharon said quietly. "I saw it. And you didn't go to her."

"No."

Slowly, proudly, Sharon walked over to him and faced him, her face radiant. "I watched it. And I'm not soft if I can do that, am I?"

Memory did not have to grope for her meaning. She came into his arms, pressing her body to him, and her kisses, warm and dear, on his lips and his face.

Bonal let himself quietly into the other room. The door closed, he stood motionless, trying to know the way love went, and his only memory dim and almost sad.